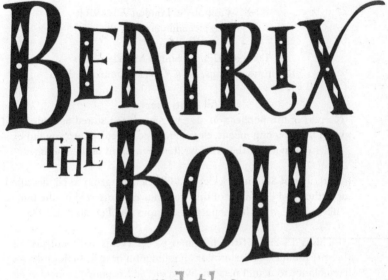

BEATRIX THE BOLD

and the BALLOON of DOOM

Simon Mockler

Piccadilly
PRESS

First published in Great Britain in 2020 by
PICCADILLY PRESS
80–81 Wimpole St, London W1G 9RE
www.piccadillypress.co.uk

A CIP catalogue record for this book is available from the British
Library.

ISBN: 978-1-84812-840-8
also available as an ebook

1
Printed and bound in Great Britain by Clays Ltd, Elcograf S.p.A.

Piccadilly Press is an imprint of Bonnier Books UK
www.bonnierbooks.co.uk

For my children

Prologue

The Curse of the Wobblers

When we last saw Beatrix the Bold, Oi the Boy and Wilfred the Wise, they had just rescued the naughty children of Riddletown from General Burpintime's marshmallow factory, dodged the flaming arrows fired by his Evil Army and floated down the fast-flowing River Riddle on marshmallow boats. They weren't supposed to do any of this – they were supposed to be on their way to Beluga, so that Beatrix could *finally* meet her parents, whom she hadn't seen since she was a tiny baby. But things never turn out quite as smoothly as you'd like, especially not when there's an Evil Army on your trail who think you're going to destroy them because of an ancient curse.

Ah, the Curse of the Wobblers. This curse has been following Beatrix around like a bad smell since she was born. (Not that Beatrix smelt bad – although it had been a few days since any of them had taken a bath. Adventures don't leave much time for things like taking baths.)

The Evil Army wanted to **kill** her because the curse said she would take over their land and their castles, and the Evil Army was a lot more dangerous than a bad smell. They were also a lot more smelly. They were more like a *really* bad smell – imagine a cheese and onion sandwich that's slipped behind the radiator and has been warming nicely for a couple of days.

This time it wasn't just Beatrix they were after, it was her whole family. And her castle. And her friends. And anyone else who got in their way. (If you ever get a whiff of a cheese and onion sandwich, drop what you're doing and run!)

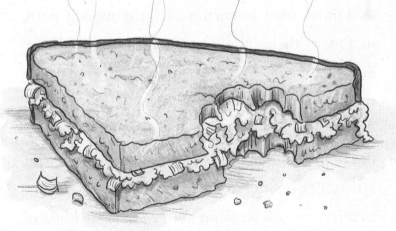

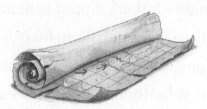

1

The Sea of Sinking Ships

It was a cold, grey day and Beatrix, Oi and Wilfred were bouncing along a muddy path, as fast as their little cart could go, towards the Sea of Sinking Ships. They were looking more than a little bedraggled. Wilfred was covered in soot and sticky bits of marshmallow. Oi had eaten the marshmallow that was stuck to him but was splattered with mud from the River Riddle. Beatrix was still wearing her *Fernando the Fantastic*

disguise, complete with cape and wizard's hat, but she looked more like a pile of old clothes than a magician. They'd been bouncing along this path for almost two days, feeling more than a little tired but too bumped about to fall asleep.

In fact, if you added together the unslept hours of **all** children on Christmas Eve, and piled this on top of them, then that's how much tiredness they were carrying around. But they couldn't stop. Not even for a moment, not even to grab a quick squashed-meatball-in-a-bun for lunch. They had to get to Collywobble-on-Sea as fast as possible so they could hire a ship to take them across the Sea of Sinking Ships to Beluga.

If they didn't get to Beluga before General Burpintime, they didn't know what he'd do. Well, they *sort of* knew what he'd do, because they'd heard him shouting VERY LOUDLY about how he'd DESTROY BEATRIX'S FAMILY AND THE CASTLE AND ALL HER FRIENDS AND ALL HER PETS (and so on) while his marshmallow factory burned to the ground. He was very angry, and even when he wasn't angry, he still liked to destroy things. So now he was in double destruction mode.

'I hope we get to the port before nightfall,' Wilfred said in a sleepy voice. 'I don't think I can face another night out in the open. I'm still shivering from last night.'

Beatrix took the map from her bag and opened it with cold, shaky hands.

'It's not much further. We should see it once we get over the top of this hill. The Sea of Sinking Ships is on the other side.'

'Do you think General Burpintime will have sent some spies there?' Oi said.

Beatrix looked at the map. 'Maybe. We'll have to be careful.' As she said this she couldn't help glancing over her shoulder. Behind her was nothing but an empty road and spindly, bare trees. 'If they were following us, we'd have seen them by now. Or heard them. If there's one thing the Evil Army isn't very good at, it's being quiet. They're always too busy arguing about cheese and onion sandwiches and things like that.'

'And the last thing General Burpintime said was…' Oi paused. He didn't really want to remind Beatrix of what General Burpintime had been shouting.

'He's going to destroy my family in Beluga?' Beatrix said. 'That's why we have to get there before him. As fast as we can. Across the Sea of Sinking Ships.'

Oi nodded. 'By the way, is the Sea of Sinking Ships actually more dangerous than other seas, or has it just got a bit of a bad reputation?' he said.

'The weather is *famously* bad,' Wilfred replied. 'They say the storms can blow up out of nowhere.'

'They say there are pirates too,' Beatrix added. 'They like to sink ships after they've stolen all the gold.'

'What about Sea Wobblers?' Oi said. 'They say they're like an ordinary Wobbler crossed with a jellyfish, so they're even more wobbly than usual. Apparently the Sea of Sinking Ships is full of them.'

'Er, I don't think there's any danger of Sea Wobblers attacking us,' Beatrix said, 'what with Sea Wobblers not actually existing. They're no more real than Wobblers. In fact, they're less real. If that's possible. Whatever the reason, I'm sure once we get there we'll find that it's not really a sea of sinking ships. It's just a normal sea that everybody thinks is more dangerous than other seas, and half the stories aren't actually true.'

In a way, Beatrix was right. Half the stories people told about the Sea of Sinking Ships *weren't* true. The problem was, the other half of the stories *were* true. And those stories were pretty bad. There were ships that returned to port without anyone on board and their sails in tatters. There were ships that simply vanished into the mysterious mists that floated over the waters. And there were at least three different lots of pirates who liked to set fire to the ships they captured and watch everyone on board jump into the sea, whilst they drank rum and placed bets on whether or not the passengers could swim.

With all this going on, it's no surprise that it was called the Sea of Sinking Ships. And it's no surprise that the port was called Collywobble-on-Sea. Winter was the worst time to sail, and winter still had two more months of storms stored up in its thundery skies, ready to unleash upon anyone foolish enough to try to sail to Beluga.

2

Collywobble-on-Sea

It was dusk by the time they got to the bottom of the hill. The flickering lanterns of Collywobble-on-Sea stood out against the darkening sky, and the town looked... well, not too bad actually. I was going to say *dark and menacing*, but it wasn't very menacing and, although it was getting dark, all the lanterns made it look quite jolly.

'I wasn't expecting it to look like this,' Beatrix said, as Wilfred stopped the cart. The entrance to

the port looked like a theme park. They could make out a big model of a wooden ship with a carved sea serpent wrapped around it and a large, smiling shark's head above the gates.

The sea serpent looked very pleased with itself and there was even a happy mermaid on the bow of the ship. A lantern swung on a pole above a sign which said "*Welcome to Collywobble-on-Sea! We hope you have a pleasant crossing*". It creaked in the wind as it swung back and forth.

'The gates aren't locked and there aren't any guards,' Beatrix said. '*Very strange.*'

On one side of the main street there were little shops and houses. They were all different sizes and were packed close together in a cosy, huddled-round-the-fire sort of way. They looked out over the harbour, which was full of fishing boats, floating silently up and down on the black water. The harbour curved round in a semi-circle and on the far side there was a much larger ship that was tied to iron rings in the harbour wall. Beatrix thought it looked a bit like an animal that had been tied up because it might try to escape.

'Look, there's an inn on the other side of the harbour,' Wilfred said.

'Let's see if we can order some dinner and find out if anyone has a ship that can take us to Beluga,' Beatrix replied. 'I quite fancy the look of that big one. It looks as if it could survive a storm or two.'

A sign above the inn said 'The Happy Plaice' and showed a picture of a smiling fish, caught on a fishing line. They could hear laughter coming from inside.

'Let me check it first for spies,' Wilfred said, peering in through the window. 'You can't be too careful.'

He couldn't see any strange-looking soldiers from the Evil Army disguised as farmers – or fishermen for that matter. Instead, he could see lots of very fine tables and chairs, chandeliers hanging from the ceiling and well-dressed customers tucking into their dinner.

'Nothing suspicious, as far as I can see. It looks very posh. Let's go in.' He held open the door for Beatrix, Oi, Dog and Jeff. (Jeff the pigeon, not Jeff the horse. Jeff the horse was still outside. Jeff the pigeon was in a cage carried by Beatrix.)

'This is more like one of the rooms at the palace than an inn,' Beatrix said as they sat down at a table by the fire. There were bronze statues on the mantlepiece and paintings hung on the walls next to mirrors in gold frames. The cushions on the seats were plump and comfy and covered in velvet.

A large lady in an apron approached the table with a piece of slate in her hand. She had a broad smile in which three gold teeth twinkled and a necklace that glittered with diamonds.

'Good evening, travellers, and welcome to Collywobble-on-Sea. Would you be after some dinner?'

'We certainly would,' Wilfred replied.

'Excellent! I can recommend the fish cakes. They're delicious.'

'I don't really like fish,' Oi said. 'Do you have anything else?'

'Nope. We only serve fish cakes. The finest fish cakes in the land.'

'OK, I'll just have the cake, then. No fish, thanks.'

The innkeeper frowned. 'One fish cake without the fish,' she repeated. The chalk she was using to write down the order squeaked across the slate.

'And how about you two?' she said, turning to Beatrix and Wilfred and attempting another smile.

'We'll have fish cakes *with* fish, please,' Beatrix replied. The innkeeper started to write down *fish cakes with fish* then crossed it out and just wrote *fish cakes*. 'Anything else?'

'Well…' Beatrix said, 'do you know who owns that big ship out in the harbour?'

'I might do,' replied the innkeeper. 'Why are you askin'?'

'Because we'd like to hire it.'

'And where would you be goin' in that big ship, at this time o' year?'

Beatrix smiled, but she didn't answer the question. The innkeeper seemed a little nosy. Instead, she said: 'Haven't decided yet. Somewhere sunny. Do you know who owns it or not?'

The woman looked at them carefully, as if they were pieces of jewellery and she was trying to work out how much they were worth.

'Well, I might do, but it's going to be very expensive because that's a very large ship and it's so dangerous at this time of year. The storms can rise up out of nowhere and sink a ship before you can say '*How do you do doggy paddle again?*'

'We're happy to pay. Whoever takes us will be well rewarded.'

The innkeeper eyed them doubtfully. They certainly didn't look as if they could afford to hire an enormous ship. She stared at Beatrix a moment longer, and she seemed to be making up her mind about something.

'I'll go and find him,' she said. 'Let's see what he says.'

3

A Ship, a Captain, and Something More Fishy than a three-day-old Fish Cake

The innkeeper returned a short while later with a tall, thin man, who was very smartly dressed. He wore long black leather boots that were a size too big and a thick black cape, with gold stitching and gold buttons, that was a size too small. On his head was a hat with three points and he had a long moustache that curled at the ends.

'Pleasure to meet you,' he said. 'I'm Captain Phil McCannonball.'

Oi, trying not to laugh, looked at Beatrix then back at the captain. '*Feel my cannonball?*' he said.

'Aye, that's what I said – Phil McCannonball. Something funny about that, is there?' An icy look came into his eye – so cold it could freeze any joke stone dead.

'Nothing at all,' Oi said with a very serious face.

'How soon can you get a crew ready to sail across the Sea of Sinking Ships?' Beatrix asked. 'We want to go to…' She leant forwards. '*Beluga,*' she said quietly.

'Beluga, eh? A lovely city,' the captain replied. 'Depends on how soon you can pay me.' He sat down, took a pipe from his pocket, pressed some tobacco into it and lit it. The smoke curled around him.

'Erm…' Beatrix felt in her pocket for the bag of gold coins they'd brought with them. They hadn't spent much in Riddletown, but she had no idea if one bag of coins would be enough to hire a ship to take them all the way to Beluga.

'Is this enough?' Beatrix said, taking out the bag and placing it on the table.

The captain picked up the bag and tested its weight with his hand. Then he shook his head. 'It'll cost a lot more than that,' he said. 'Especially at this time of year.'

'We could pay you more when we get to Beluga,' Wilfred said. 'We're a family of travelling magicians and we've got a whole series of magic shows lined up, and they're sure to be a success.'

'You don't look like you get paid very well,' the captain said, with a sly look on his face as he peered at them through the pipe smoke. 'What's the name of this magic troupe of yours?'

'Bob the Magician's Amazing Magic Show,' Wilfred replied. 'I'm Bob. These are my two assistants.'

The captain looked at the three of them a moment longer. He was clearly suspicious about something. 'I'll be back in a moment,' he said. He got up and walked to the counter at the back of the inn.

'What's he doing?' Oi said.

'Not sure – I can't quite see,' Beatrix replied, standing up to get a better view. 'He's talking to the innkeeper. Looks as if they're discussing something. They're both nodding.'

Then the captain walked back to their table. 'I think that bag of gold will be enough after all,' he said. 'You can pay me the rest when we get to Beluga.'

'Amazing. Thank you. How long will it take to get there?' Beatrix asked.

'With a fair wind and a flat sea I'll have you in Beluga in seven days.'

'And we set sail tomorrow?'

'Aye. I'll need to order the supplies and get the

crew ready, but I'll make a start at first light and we should be on our way by midday.' The captain shook their hands, then raised his hat.

'If you don't mind,' he went on, 'I'll be taking this too.' He whipped the bag of gold coins off the table. 'See you in the morn, bright and early.'

'Well, we have a ship. And a captain,' Beatrix said, watching Captain McCannonball walk away.

'We do. It seemed very easy to organise,' Oi added.

'Sometimes things just work out the way you want them to.' Wilfred sat back in his chair and rested his feet on a log near the fire. 'After all the bad luck we've had, I'm not surprised things are going our way. It's only right that we have a little good fortune. That's how the world works. Day follows night. Spring follows winter. Pudding follows sprouts.'

Beatrix stared into the fire. She hoped Wilfred

was right, but she couldn't help thinking there was something strange about Collywobble-on-Sea, with all its fine decorations, its fancy fish cakes, and its smiling, smartly-dressed captain, whose clothes didn't quite fit. They would have to be on their guard. Once you were on a ship, there was no way to escape. Unless, of course, you wanted to go for a very long swim.

4

The *Cutty Shark*

The next morning was bright and cold and the sea was as flat as one of the big silver plates that Beatrix, Oi and Wilfred were eating their breakfast off in The Happy Plaice. It was fish cakes again, which meant it was not a very happy place to eat breakfast, but at least there were some freshly baked rolls to go with the fish cakes. After breakfast they packed their bags onto the cart and went to find the captain's ship.

The *Cutty Shark* was moored on the far side of the harbour. It looked strong and sturdy, but it wasn't what you'd call a beautiful ship. The way it sat low in the water reminded Beatrix of a bulldog. The hull was painted black, and there were patches of fresh paint where it had been recently repaired.

The crew were busy checking the sails and doing funny things with ropes, as well as grunting and muttering sailory things like '*Stick this starboard, not port side.*'

'You'll have to leave the horse,' Captain McCannonball called out from the deck. 'One of the fishermen will look after him. You can't take horses on ships.'

'Why not?' Beatrix shouted back. 'It's a big ship.'

'It's against the rules.'

'What rules?'

'The rules that say you can't have horses on a ship. They get seasick. *Very* seasick. And then they go mad because they're feeling sick and start kicking things and kick a hole in the ship. It's *very* dangerous and *very* messy.'

Beatrix climbed down from the cart.

'Looks like we'll have to leave you,' she said, patting Jeff on the nose. 'But we'll find someone nice to look after you. Right! Oi, Wilfred, let's get everything loaded onto the ship.'

A short while later they were standing on the main deck, waiting for the crew to take their things to their cabin.

'Do all ships do this?' Oi said.

'Do what?' Beatrix replied.

'Move up and down.'

'Of course they do. And we're in the harbour. We're barely moving up and down at all. It's more like a gentle rocking. You were fine on a marshmallow boat, and that was moving all over the place.'

'Yes, but moving all over the place and moving a little bit are very different. This is making me feel like I'm going to see my breakfast again. And I've had quite enough of fish cakes – they still taste a bit fishy even without the fish, and a fishy cake is not a good thing.'

'How are you this morning?' Captain McCannonball said, ducking under one of the sails and slapping Oi on the back. 'You're looking a little

green, my boy. Here, chew this.' He passed Oi a couple of sprigs of mint. 'Shouldn't be long now before we're off,' the captain went on cheerfully. 'There's a good easterly wind which we can catch.'

Beatrix noticed that once again he was very well-dressed. Today he wore a bright red coat with a fur collar and a different pair of boots, with golden buckles. This time the coat was a little large on him, and the boots were a little small.

'How do you know which way

to go?' she asked. All she could see was a vast ocean of silvery blue and a horizon of bluey silver.

Captain McCannonball placed his hands on his hips and drew a deep breath of sea air.

'Lots of charts, my dear, and special measuring instruments. We check the speed of the ship using a knotted rope we hang over the side, then I work out the distance we've gone from that. It's not a hundred per cent accurate but it's pretty good. And there are certain rocks and islands we should pass along the way, so we know we're going in the right direction. For example, in three days, we'll reach Devil Sprout Island. If we haven't reached it, then I know I've gone the wrong way, and we'll turn around and go back the way we came and try again.'

'How do you know the way back?' Beatrix asked.

'Why, that's easy, it's behind us,' the captain replied.

'How do you know the right way forwards once you've gone back?'

'That's even easier, we go a little more to the left or to the right of where we went last time.'

'What if you get it wrong?'

'Then we try again.'

'Sounds like it's a bit hit and miss. What if the wind blows you off course?'

'What if, what if...' The captain frowned. 'Do you *always* ask this many questions?'

'I ask as many questions as it takes to get the right answer,' Beatrix replied. 'Sometimes more. Sometimes less. Depends who's doing the answering.'

'If the wind blows us off course then we're off course. But don't worry, I've only missed Devil Sprout Island once. And it doesn't really matter if you do miss it. If you keep on sailing you'll always end up somewhere. *Eventually.* The portions get a bit smaller at meal times and you might find yourself dreaming of a nice glass of water once that runs out, but you'll find land eventually. *Usually.*' He drew in another deep breath of sea air.

'So you see, nothing to worry about. The sea is like an old friend to me. And if she decides to be mean, gets in a temper and rolls us over, then we always have the lifeboat.' He pointed to the back of the ship, where a rowing boat was tied to the wooden rails that ran round the deck.

Beatrix looked at the boat. She was pretty sure they wouldn't be able to fit the whole crew in if anything went wrong.

'Why's it called Devil Sprout Island?' Oi asked.

'Because nothing grows there except sprouts,' the captain replied. 'Nasty-tasting sprouts. Even worse than usual. If you get shipwrecked on that desolate place you might as well give up all hope. There's many a tale of sailors shipwrecked on that island that have gone mad from eating only sprouts.'

'Not surprised,' Oi said. 'They're bad enough on the side of the plate – you don't want them taking up the middle as well. Sprouts for every meal, day after day after day…' Oi's face started to turn green again. He took a mint leaf from his pocket and chewed it. This one had a bit of marshmallow stuck to it, so it tasted better.

Captain McCannonball looked over the side of the ship at the water. He stared at it for a while, as if he was reading a page in a book with a lot of difficult words on it.

'The weather's calm now, but it won't be so good once we approach the waters around Devil Sprout Island,' he said. 'It's always bad there. Mists roll down from the mountains and spread out over the sea so you can't see the rocks.' He stared straight ahead. 'Aye, there'll be dangers ahead, and no mistake.' Then he smiled his creepy smile, rubbed his hands together and said, 'Shall I show you to your cabin?'

5

Oi has a Funny Feeling
(and Not Just because he's Seasick)

Beatrix, Oi and Wilfred followed the captain. He led them down wooden steps and along a narrow corridor with lots of doors leading off it.

'You have to be careful on a ship this big, you can get lost easily. If you got stuck in one of the storerooms in the hull we might never find you. So, no exploring. That's my only rule. Well, not my *only* rule. No horses, no jumping in the sea, no running on the deck when it's wet, no fires apart from in the stoves, no singing.'

'Why no singing?' Beatrix said.

'It attracts the sharks,' said the captain.

'What… how?'

'Because I hate singing, and if anyone sings I throw them in the sea and that attracts the sharks – ha ha ha!'

Beatrix, Oi and Wilfred stared at the captain.

'*Joke*!' he said, then, more quietly: 'But seriously,

no singing. I don't like it. Now, follow me to your cabin.'

Captain McCannonball opened the door at the end of the corridor to reveal a large room with three comfy-looking hammocks, a stove with a pot on it for boiling water, and a couple of armchairs.

'I wasn't expecting this,' Beatrix said, as she looked round the room.

'Nor was I,' Wilfred said. 'Looks like we'll be travelling in comfort the rest of the way.'

The captain smiled at them. 'You see this cord here?' he said, pointing at a piece of fine silk, attached to a rope that hung by the door. 'Pull this whenever you want anything and we'll bring it to you. Some wood for your stove, a glass of milk and honey. Just don't go exploring.'

With that, Captain McCannonball twirled the end of his moustache, performed a small bow and left the room, the smile permanently fixed to his face, a bit like his moustache.

'Well, this really is the way to travel,' Wilfred said, relaxing in an armchair. 'I can't believe we tried going over the mountains. What's the matter, Oi, you're not still feeling seasick are you?'

'I am a bit, but there's something else. A funny feeling I can't shake.' Oi looked around the room, then said: 'When I was younger, my brothers always used to say things like, *Why don't you go in that cave, it's full of marshmallows*, then, when I'd go in, there'd be an angry bear who'd chase me away. Or they'd say, *Come for a swim with us in the lake, it's lovely and warm*. Then the water would be freezing and they'd steal my clothes.'

'I know what you mean,' Beatrix said. 'It all seems a little too good to be true. If a dragon turns up and acts all friendly, then asks if you want to go to a party and have an endless supply of sweets, you may well end up working day and night in a marshmallow factory.'

Beatrix looked out of the porthole. A voice on

the shore called out 'Cast her off!' She watched the sailors untie the ropes and heard the rattle of the chain as the anchor was pulled up. The wooden ship creaked as it pulled away from the shore. They felt it surge forward as the wind filled the sails. There was no turning back now.

We'll be in Beluga in a week, Beatrix told herself. *And I'll finally see my parents and I'll be able to warn them about General Burpintime and Esmerelda.*

She put all other thoughts out of her head. Or at least she tried to. But bad thoughts are like boomerangs. You throw them away and they spin back round and whack you on the back of the head when you're least expecting it. There was something not quite right about the captain and his ship, and this bad thought had just spun back and donked her on the head again.

6

A Marshmallow a Day...
is Never Enough!

On a faraway mountain top, General Burpintime and Esmerelda the Terrible looked towards the horizon. It was a cold, clear day. The wind ruffled General Burpintime's ginger moustache as he squinted into the bright light. It looked like a shivering squirrel on his top lip. They had spent three days trekking through the mountains. So far, there had been one avalanche – which had only just missed them – and two snow storms. In front of

them were snow-filled valleys and dangerous cliffs, dense woods and an icy river.

And behind them were ten thousand soldiers from the Evil Army pretending they didn't feel cold. (No soldier in the Evil Army could ever admit to feeling cold, or afraid, or sad – or even happy, for that matter.) They were only allowed to be angry so, at the moment, they were having angry snowball fights and building angry-looking snowmen on the mountainside as they waited for General Burpintime and Esmerelda the Terrible to decide which way to go. Some of them had even brewed up nice, warming cups of hot chocolate, and were drinking it angrily.

'Well,' General Burpintime said to Esmerelda. 'How much further is it to your sister's palace in Beluga?'

'That depends,' Esmerelda said in her haughty voice, pulling her fur coat closer around her shoulders.

'What does it depend on?' General Burpintime said, blowing into his hands.

'On whether you brought horse skis.'

'You mean *huskies*,' General Burpintime replied. 'Huskies would be useful for pulling the sledges, but they're very yappy and I'm not really a dog person. I don't like any animals. Except possibly guinea pigs.'

'I don't mean *huskies*,' Esmerelda replied coldly. 'I mean horse skis. Skis for horses.'

General Burpintime looked behind him at the shivering horses.

'I did not bring horse skis. Horse skis do not exist.'

'Well, they should. They make shoes for horses, so why not skis? Without horse skis, it will take us another week and a half to get to Beluga. Which means Beatrix might beat us. It'll only take her seven days by ship if the weather stays like this. If we had horse skis, we'd get there much more quickly.'

'There is no such thing as a horse ski,' General

Burpintime hissed under his breath. 'I doubt she'll even get to Beluga,' he said, aloud. 'I've sent spies to all the ports and towns along the way. I'm offering a reward of ten thousand gold coins to anyone who captures her and brings her to my castle. None of those greedy captains will take her to Beluga. Not when they could get all that gold from me. And if she does somehow make it, we'll be there first. Even without horse skis.'

He thrust his hands into his pockets. He had four marshmallows left. Two in each pocket. He felt them with his fingers. All nice and soft and ready to be eaten.

You must be strong, he told himself. He let go of the marshmallows and took his hands out of his pockets. He was saving them for emergencies. Now that he didn't have a factory producing an endless supply, he had to eat them much more slowly. One at a time. Sometimes even only half at a time. He only had seven more boxes with him. There were twenty in each box, that was one hundred and forty. They needed to last him all the way to Beluga, through the length of the battle and the journey home, which was approximately thirty days in total. So, if you divided one hundred and forty by thirty, you got...Hang on. He scratched his head. Four? No, that would mean he had one hundred and twenty. Just over four, then. He could eat four a day. That was fine. And today he'd only had two with breakfast, then one in a hot chocolate to sweeten it a bit, one as a mid-morning snack, one as a pre-lunch snack and two with lunch to make the cheese and onion sandwiches taste better. That meant he'd already eaten... he held up his fingers, *One, two... four, six, seven.*

'What on earth are you doing?' Esmerelda said, looking at the fingers Burpintime was holding up in front of his face.

'What? Oh, nothing,' Burpintime replied. 'Well, not nothing. Some very complicated mathematics. There is a lot to organise, in case you hadn't noticed. I'm under a lot of pressure. If I don't capture Beatrix this time, the Evil Overlord is going to kill me. And probably you as well, because you're not exactly a great help.'

'Well as long as you can work out how to do all that with eight fingers, it can't be too complicated.'

General Burpintime's face went red. He stuffed a hand in his pocket, pulled out two marshmallows and shoved them both into his mouth.

'And don't eat all those marshmallows at once. You'll run out. And then you'll be even more grumpy. Now, shall we go over my plan to take over my sister's castle one last time? I don't want you to mess things up again. We all remember what happened to your marshmallow factory. And your dragon costume.'

7

Beatrix, Oi and Wilfred Get Suspicious

The first two days of sailing passed uneventfully, which was a tiny bit disappointing for Beatrix, Oi and Wilfred, after all the talk of storms and Sea Wobblers and pirates. The captain brought their meals to their cabin, and was always friendly (in his slightly creepy way). To pass the time they would walk around the deck and play battleships and hangman and a game Oi invented called Spot the Shark. So far, no one had seen a shark.

That was because there weren't any sharks in the Sea of Sinking Ships. There wasn't even anything that looked like a shark, which meant it was a very boring  game. A bit like 'I spy' played in the dark.

Beatrix tried talking to the crew but whenever she appeared they would stop their card playing and joking and find a section of deck that needed cleaning or a knot that needed tying, or untying. Sometimes the same knot.

'Why do you keep tying and untying that knot?' Beatrix asked one of the sailors, after lunch on the third day. The man looked at the knot, then looked at Beatrix.

'Just checking it's knotted,' he said.

'By untying it?'

'Er, yeah.' The sailor kept staring at the knot.

'How far are we from Beluga?' she asked.

The sailor shrugged. 'Few more days, depending on the wind,' he said. He put the rope down, got up and walked to the other side of the ship.

'The crew aren't very friendly,' Beatrix said to Oi and Wilfred later, as they sat in their cabin. 'They won't really talk to me.'

'Me neither,' said Oi. 'When I try and ask them anything they either ignore me or walk away. It's as if they're hiding something.'

'I'm sure they're just very busy,' Wilfred said. 'Sometimes grown-ups don't like talking to children when they're trying to work.'

'They weren't working. They were playing cards,' Beatrix said. 'Do they talk to you?' she asked.

Wilfred frowned. 'Actually no, now you come to mention it. They haven't even asked me to perform any magic tricks, which is most odd. Normally it's the first thing people ask when you say you're a magician.'

'I think Oi might be right,' Beatrix said.
'It definitely feels as if they're trying to hide
something. Also, have you noticed Jeff's cage?'

'What about it?' said Wilfred.

'Have a look.'

'Um, it's not quite hanging straight down, it's
sort of wonky,' Oi said.

'It is hanging straight down,' Beatrix replied,
'it's the ship that's tilting ever so slightly to one

side. It's been tilting that way since this morning.'

'Which means what, exactly?' Oi asked.

'We're turning, very slowly. We're turning away from Beluga. I'm going to ask the captain where we're going. He said we go straight to Beluga, past Devil Sprout Island. He didn't say anything about turning once we'd got halfway.'

She pulled the cord and rang the bell. Captain McCannonball appeared a few moments later. As usual he was dressed in very fine clothes, and as usual they didn't quite fit him.

'How are we today, my favourite shipmates?' he asked in a cheerful voice.

'Very well thank you, Captain. Tell me, I have a feeling the ship is turning slightly – are we taking a different route to Beluga?'

The captain smiled an even bigger smile.

'What a bright young lady you are – just like everybody says. There's a storm coming and I wanted to run a little to the north, back towards the shore. Just for safety. The waters are always calmer there. I don't want my beautiful ship to end up at the bottom of the sea. Or any of you, for that matter. Anything else I can help you with?' The captain twirled his moustache.

'No, that's all. Thank you.'

'Well, just ring the bell if you need me.' He bowed as he left the room.

'Did you hear what he said?' Beatrix asked, once he was gone.

'There's a storm coming and we need to sail closer to the shore,' Wilfred said.

'Not that bit. The bit where he said I was a bright young lady, *just like everybody says*. Why would he say that? Who says I'm bright?'

'Well, you're Beatrix the Bold, everyone knows you're super intelligent.'

'How would he know I'm Beatrix the Bold?! He thinks I'm an assistant to Bob the Amazing Magician.'

Wilfred scratched his head. He hoped an answer would pop into it, but it didn't, so he scratched his bottom instead. An answer didn't pop into that either. Or out of it.

'That might not be exactly what he meant,' he said at last. 'Perhaps some of the crew said they thought you were clever.'

'Doubt it. They've barely spoken to me. I think we need to explore the ship,' Beatrix said. 'I don't trust McCannonball. I want to know why we've changed direction.'

'But he specifically told us *not* to explore the ship,' Wilfred said.

'Exactly,' Beatrix said. 'All the more reason to search it. If there's one thing I hate it's being told I can't go in certain rooms.'

8

Oi's Favourite
Cannonball Joke

Later that night, Beatrix, Oi, Wilfred and Dog left their cabin and crept down the narrow steps into the hull of the ship. The storm Captain McCannonball had warned them about was brewing outside and he was on the deck with the crew, taking down the sails and fastening everything on deck so it wouldn't blow away.

It smelt musty and damp below deck. There were piles of material, and thick rope coiled like sleeping snakes next to them.

'This must be where they store the canvas to fix the sails,' Beatrix said, lifting up some of the material. 'That's strange,' she said. Underneath the sail was a wooden wheel attached to a big wooden box. She pulled the rest of the canvas away, to reveal three more wheels and a long, heavy metal pipe on top of the box.

'That is most definitely a cannon,' Beatrix said.

'Indeed it is,' Oi said.

'Quite a big one,' Wilfred added.

Beatrix lifted another canvas sheet. 'There's another one here,' she said. 'Cannons in disguise. Very strange – on a passenger ship. Let's see what else the captain is hiding. I want to find his cabin.'

They descended another set of stairs, further into the ship. The wood creaked beneath their feet as the ship rose and fell on the waves. The further they went, the darker it became. They lit lanterns so they could see the way. The corridor was narrow. There were several doors and they all had "Supplies – NO ENTRY" written on them. Beatrix tried one of the doors. It opened with a loud creak.

'Barrels of food, water, biscuits, ham and –'

'Pickled sprouts?!' Oi said, reading the label on one of the barrels.

They tried another door. More supplies.

'The captain is certainly well prepared,' Wilfred said, looking round the room. 'It's only a seven-day voyage but there's enough food here to keep us going for months.'

They walked along the narrow corridor to the rear of the ship. At the end was a door with a sign that said 'Captain McCannonball's Cabin – NO ENTRY.'

'Looks like we've found it,' Beatrix said. 'Where's McCannonball?'

'Where's your cannonball?' Oi asked.

'No – where's *Captain McCannonball?* Are you going to make that joke every time someone says "Where's McCannonball"?'

'Possibly,' Oi replied. 'It's my second favourite cannonball joke.'

'What's your favourite?' Beatrix asked.

'The pirate wondered why the cannonball was getting bigger, and then it hit him! Anyway, McCannonball's busy. He'll be battening down the hatches and all the other sailory things you have to do before a storm.'

The ship lurched beneath them and Wilfred almost lost his balance. Beatrix tried the door. 'Locked,' she said. 'Wilfred, you'll need to use one of your magic tricks to open it.'

'Of course,' Wilfred said. 'I'll use the magic trick with the two pieces of metal that can fit in any lock and open it. Stand back please…' He placed his hands over the keyhole, waved them about so that the door rattled, then turned the handle. Then he put his 'magic' keys back in his pocket.

'There we go,' he said, opening the door. 'Goodness!' He drew a deep breath. They all did.

'Wow,' said Beatrix. 'This is even more luxurious than The Happy Plaice.'

'Certainly is,' said Oi.

Dog didn't say anything, he just did a sort of doggy shrug. He preferred being outdoors.

The captain's cabin was richly decorated

indeed, with a magnificent desk in the middle and tapestries hanging on the walls. Maps and papers were laid out on the desk and finely woven rugs covered the floor.

Beatrix and Wilfred examined the maps. The top one showed the port of Collywobble-on-Sea, the Sea of Sinking Ships and Devil Sprout Island in the middle. Beluga was further along the coast on the far side. The coastline was labelled with things like *Smuggler's Cove*, *Ambush Bay*, *Dead Man's Cave* and *Secret Meeting Point*.

'Is this a normal map?' Oi asked. 'I don't think our map has any names like that on it.'

'It's a normal sailor's map,' Wilfred said, staring at it. 'You know how sailors often have different words for things?'

Beatrix frowned. 'I think the words for "ambush", "secret" and "dead man" are the same whoever's making the map.'

She stood back to get a better look, working

out how far they'd come. 'If it takes seven days to get to Beluga, and we've been travelling for three, then we should be about here.' She pointed at the map. 'Which means we're close to Devil Sprout Island, and only another four days from Beluga. But if I'm correct, and the ship really is slowly turning to the right –'

'You mean starboard,' Oi said.

'– then we're heading towards "Secret Meeting Point", which isn't anywhere near Beluga – it's a few miles along the coast from Collywobble-on-Sea.'

'Why would we be going to the Secret Meeting Point?' Oi asked.

Before anyone could reply a shrill voice shouted: 'WHAT ARE YE DOING?'

All three of them jumped and spun round. There was no one behind them.

'Who was that?' Oi said with a shudder.

'GET AWAY GET AWAY!' it screeched again.

'It's inside the room!' Beatrix exclaimed. 'It's coming from over there.'

On a table in the corner of the room was a large cage with a sheet over it. Beatrix ran towards it and pulled off the sheet.

Sitting in the cage on a perch was a beautiful macaw parrot. Its feathers were a dazzlingly bright blue and red and it looked impossibly exotic.

'What an incredible bird!' Wilfred said eventually.

'Amazing,' Beatrix agreed. 'Poor thing, stuck down here on its own.'

For a moment they forgot all about searching the captain's cabin, till Oi said: 'I don't mean to be funny. But isn't it usually pirates who keep parrots? They sit on their shoulders and says things like *Pieces of eight.*'

The parrot cocked its head on one side, and gave them a very parroty look.

'So far this one hasn't said that,' Wilfred replied. 'So maybe it's not a pirate parrot.'

'WALK THE PLANK! WALK THE PLANK!' the voice screeched.

'OK, that does sound a bit more piratey,' Wilfred admitted.

Beatrix hurried back to the desk, looking through the papers and maps. As she did so she heard the parrot squawk:

'*Ten thousand gold coins for Beatrix the Bold!*'

She stopped. 'What did it just say? *Ten thousand gold coins for Beatrix the Bold?*'

'*Dead or alive,*' the parrot added.

'*Dead or alive?!*'

'*Stop repeating everything I say,*' the parrot cackled. It really was rather a rude parrot.

At the bottom of the pile of papers, Beatrix found a drawing of a young girl. She stared at it. The face stared back at her. She felt as if she was looking at her own face in the back of a spoon.

'Look at this!' she said. Oi and Wilfred looked at the picture. 'Just like the parrot said,' she went on.

WANTED

BEATRIX THE BOLD
By order of the Evil Army
10,000 gold coins for whoever
brings her to the Evil Army Castle

DEAD OR ALIVE

Footsteps tip-tapped across the floor above them. The three of them stood very still. Dog's ears pricked up and he growled softly.

'Someone's coming!' Beatrix said.

The footsteps grew louder, coming down the stairs. She slipped the piece of paper back under the maps and charts, then threw the sheet over the parrot's cage. They hurried out of the room, locking the door shut behind them.

'So you see, this is exactly the kind of room we shouldn't go into,' Beatrix said loudly to Oi and Wilfred. 'Oh, hello, Captain. I didn't see you there.'

The captain stood with his hands on his hips.

'Well well well,' said the captain. 'How strange to find you three down here. What was the one thing I told you not to do?'

'Not sing because it attracts the sharks?' Oi said.

'The other thing.'

'Not run on the deck when it's wet?' Beatrix said.

'The other thing.'

'Not to climb the –'

'I said *Don't go exploring*,' Captain McCannonball interrupted.

'Oh, that,' Beatrix said. 'Well, I wouldn't say we were exploring, exactly. We just went the wrong way when we came out of our cabin. Down instead of up.'

'Well you can go on up again then, can't you?' the captain said, following them up the stairs, his eyes narrowed. 'The seas are getting rough. I would suggest you stay in your cabin tonight.'

'Good idea,' Beatrix said. 'You can't be too careful.'

He smiled as he closed the door of their cabin, then said:

'I'll lock it too, just so you're nice and safe.' They heard the sound of his key turning in the lock.

Beatrix waited till his footsteps had faded away. 'We need to get off this ship,' she whispered in an urgent voice.

'How?' Oi replied. 'We can't swim to shore.'

'The lifeboat?' Beatrix suggested.

'I don't fancy our chances of getting all the way back to shore in that tiny dinghy,' Wilfred said.

'We don't have to get to the shore – we're close to Devil Sprout Island. We could load up the dinghy with supplies and see if we can row there, then wait for a passing ship.'

A huge wave crashed against the side of the *Cutty Shark* and it rolled to one side, the three of them slid across the cabin, then back again as the ship righted itself.

Oi clutched his stomach, his face turning green. 'Shall we wait for the storm to pass before trying to get away?' he said.

Beatrix shook her head. 'This storm could be just what we need. The crew will be busy all night trying to fight it. With a little luck we can load up the lifeboat with supplies and slip away without them noticing.'

It wasn't just Oi who had turned green. Jeff the pigeon had turned green too. So green, he looked like he was doing an impression of McCannonball's parrot.

9

Horse Skis (not Huskies)

Whilst Oi, Wilfred, Beatrix, Dog and Jeff were planning their escape, Esmerelda the Terrible was busy ordering the soldiers in the Evil Army to chop down trees and make them into horse skis. General Burpintime had argued and argued with Esmerelda on this point, but she wouldn't listen, and in the end he decided the only way to resolve the argument was to let her make some horse skis and race her to the bottom of the mountain. He would take the traditional approach of walking very carefully so as not to fall over. Esmerelda could take the more risky approach of speeding down the mountain on the back of a horse wearing skis. Ideally, she would crash into a tree or river long before she got to the bottom of the mountain, and he could have a good laugh at her expense.

'What's your sister's castle like?' General Burpintime said, watching as Esmerelda bossed his soldiers about. He had to admit she was pretty good at getting people to do things they didn't want to do. 'I imagine it is not as large or as fancy as mine,' he added.

'Oh, it's much bigger,' Esmerelda said breezily, smacking one of the Evil Army soldiers on the back of the head as he walked past. The soldier was carrying a *very* heavy-looking tree trunk. 'You're going too slowly!' she called out after him. 'Hurry along. Chop chop!' She clapped her hands together.

The soldier turned his head and looked at Burpintime as if to say *Seriously?*

'But I imagine the inside of her castle isn't as nicely decorated as my palace. I mean, my dining room is very large, and I doubt there's a castle in the land that has special buckets to use as toilets, like I do.'

'Actually, my sister's palace is very grand. There's gold in the hills of Beluga, so she is very rich. They have the very latest in toilet-bucket technology, with a handle and everything so you can pick it up and empty it out of the window yourself. And they're made of gold. As for dining rooms, they have one for breakfast, one for lunch, one for dinner, one for afternoon snacks and one for their pets. Each of their pets. They have two cats and a monkey. That's three more dining rooms that they don't even use. Why are you so interested in what my sister's palace looks like?'

'I'm not. I mean, I'm just a curious fellow. We'll need to scale the castle walls. We'll need ladders. You'll have to draw a plan for me so we can find the best way in, take over the castle and wait for Beatrix.'

'Your army would never be able to take my sister's castle,' Esmerelda replied. 'The walls are too high and too thick. It's not like my old palace, where all you needed was a good run-up to break down the gates.'

'Then why are we –' General Burpintime started to speak, but he was interrupted by one of the soldiers.

'The skis are ready. So are the horses,' he said. Esmerelda and Burpintime looked in the direction the soldier was pointing. A row of very nervous-looking horses was standing at the top of the hill, with even more nervous-looking riders sitting on them.

'Don't worry about scaling the walls. I have a

much better idea,' Esmerelda said. She strode over to one of the horses, patted it on the neck, checked its skis were tied tightly to its hooves, then climbed onto its back.

'You won't have to attack the castle. I'll simply knock on the door and they'll let me in. I'll make up some story about wanting to see them, you know, the sort of kind thing normal people who aren't evil say. I doubt they'll have heard about your attempt to kidnap Beatrix, but even if they have, I'll say I'm really sorry and I'm there to warn them that you're coming to kill them. It's easy to tell lies to nice people because they want to believe you're as nice as they are, so they don't think you're lying. Silly really. *Much* harder to lie to a liar. Anyway, once I'm in the castle and I've had a good dinner and warmed up a bit, I'll open the doors to let you and your army in.'

'You better,' he said. 'Now then. Are you ready?' He stood back and looked at Esmerelda, sitting

high on the horse; all proud, as if it was her Evil Army, not his.

'No, I still need to –'

General Burpintime didn't let her finish the sentence.

'Good good,' he said, giving the horse a shove so it slid over the top of the mountain, the skis sliding smoothly over the soft snow as Esmerelda gripped as tightly as she could to the reins.

'I said I wasn't reeeeeeeeeaaaaady!' Esmerelda called out, as she slid away.

'See you at the bottom!' he shouted after her, 'Don't fall off!'

10

A Very Stormy Storm

It didn't take Wilfred long to unlock the cabin door with his special keys. He opened it cautiously and peered into the corridor. No one there. The lanterns along the wall swayed to and fro as the boat moved up and down on the waves.

'Let's have a look on deck before we start carrying supplies up to the boat,' Beatrix said. 'If the captain finds out what we're doing he won't just lock us in our room, he'll probably chain us up somewhere in the hold.'

'Next to a cannon,' Oi said. 'And then he'll fire the cannon.'

'Well, let's be extra careful,' Wilfred said. 'I don't think I'll look any better with a hole in my tummy.'

The ship was now rolling about on the waves like a fairground ride gone mad, and even climbing the stairs to the deck was difficult. Beatrix pushed open the door, fighting against the wind, and looked through the crack to see where the sailors were.

Above the roar of the wind, they could hear the shouts of the captain and the crew. Lightning split the sky and for a second they could see them all at the far end of the ship, working furiously to fix one of the masts.

'We need something to distract them so they don't notice us carrying everything to the lifeboat,' Beatrix said, looking around.

'If we can get Dog to chew through those ropes, those barrels will roll all over the deck. That should keep them busy,' Oi said, pointing at the stack of water barrels that were bound together near where the captain and his crew were working.

'And with any luck they'll knock some of the sailors into the sea, like a game of pirate skittles,' Wilfred added.

Oi bent down next to Dog. 'Dog, you see those ropes?'

Dog looked at the ropes, then waggled his left ear. Yes, he could see the ropes.

'I want you to chew through them.'

Dog raised an eyebrow and stared at Oi without moving. This meant he didn't understand. Oi made a chewing face and growled. Dog raised the other eyebrow. This meant he still didn't understand.

'The ropes,' Oi said. 'Attack the ropes. Bad ropes!'

Bad ropes? Dog jumped up, barked and ran in a small circle. He scampered across the deck towards the barrels, then began to gnaw on the thick ropes holding them in place. It didn't take long before the rope started to fray. He chewed furiously through the last few strands and the barrels broke free, crashing onto the deck. They rolled towards the crew as the ship lurched downwards. Dog darted back towards them, skidding across the slippery planks.

'Pirate skittles!' Oi said, watching as the startled crew tried to jump out of the way.

'Come on, we don't have much time,' Beatrix said. 'Let's get those supplies. As much as we can carry.'

The three of them worked hard, fighting against the roll of the ship. They dragged up supplies from the store rooms – crates and boxes labelled with Ham, Biscuits and Crackers (Very Dry), and loaded them into the little boat. They could still hear the pirates shouting at the other end of the ship as they tried to stop the barrels rolling all over the place.

'One of us is going to have to untie the ropes and lower the lifeboat into the sea,' Wilfred said.

'I'll do it,' Beatrix replied. 'You and Oi get in, with Dog and Jeff. Once you're in the water I'll jump down.'

Wilfred was about to argue with her and tell her that was far too dangerous, but he could see her face was set. Also, she was much better at doing things like jumping and climbing than him. He climbed into the boat with Oi, his hands holding onto the sides. Beatrix unfastened the ropes that stopped the lifeboat from banging into the ship, then started to turn the handle to lower it into the water. It was stiff and she could hardly get it to move. She gritted her teeth and pushed as hard as she could and at last it gave way. Slowly, the little boat descended. With each turn it edged closer to the angry sea, swinging in the wind and knocking against the ship. Oi and Wilfred clung onto the sides, hoping they wouldn't be tipped overboard.

A voice carried on the wind. An extremely angry voice:

'What are you doing? Where do you think you're going?!'

Beatrix turned. Captain McCannonball was heading towards her, sliding on the deck. If it hadn't been for the storm he would have been there in seconds, but the ship kept rolling up and down, sending him backwards and forwards.

Beatrix took out one of her throwing knives. No time for winding the boat gently down into the sea. She hacked at the rope instead – it was thick and stiff with salt but the little knife made short work of it. She cut through the final few strands and the lifeboat dropped the last metre, hitting the water with a splash and soaking Oi, Wilfred, Dog and Jeff.

The captain lurched towards her, slipping on the wet wood. He pulled out his sword.

'Get back here, *Beatrix the Bold*!' There was no

smile on his face now. 'I'll deliver you to the Evil Army – dead or alive!' He lifted his arm, ready to swing the sword. Beatrix threw her knife, quick as a flash, pinning his sleeve to the stack of wooden barrels behind him. With his free hand he struggled to pull it out, and by the time he had, Beatrix was gone.

She jumped over the side of the ship and into the lifeboat, nimble as a cat that has just won the gold medal for cat nimbleness at the Cat Olympics.

'Hold on tight!' shouted Wilfred, grabbing hold of the oars and steering them away from the pirate ship. 'It's going to be a rough few hours.'

He was right – the next few hours were the most terrifying Beatrix, Oi and Wilfred had ever known. The lifeboat rose and fell on the waves and they felt as if it could capsize at any instant; they were soaked by the rain and blasted by the icy wind. They were cold, wet and uncertain whether they would ever reach land again, let alone Beluga.

But storms do not last for ever. Even the fiercest weather eventually tires of being stormy. Like an angry toddler that's thrown a tantrum in a supermarket then falls asleep as if nothing ever happened, so does a storm.

As daylight broke over the Sea of Sinking Ships, the waters grew tired of throwing everyone around and began to settle down. The *Cutty Shark* was nowhere to be seen, and Beatrix, Oi and Wilfred

caught sight of an island in the distance. It sat on the horizon like a misshapen hat.

'Must be Devil Sprout Island,' Beatrix said in a

shivery voice. They rowed towards it, pulling with tired arms against the current. All day long they rowed, barely speaking, thinking how *wonderful* it would be to be back on dry land; thinking that if they didn't make it, they could get caught in another storm, and they might not be so lucky next time. As they drew closer they felt the waves carry their little boat towards the beach. For once the sea was on their side, helping them reach the shore, lifting them up on its shoulders.

At last, too tired to even speak, and with all their muscles aching, the boat washed up on the stony beach.

'Phew,' said Oi.

'Woof,' said Dog.

'I don't think I ever want to go on a ship again,' Wilfred said.

'Apart from the one that rescues us,' Beatrix replied, looking out to sea.

Jeff looked around and did one of his pigeony

shrugs, then nestled his beak under his wing and went back to sleep.

Behind the beach was a forest and in the middle of the forest was a mountain that had once been a volcano.

Oi looked puzzled.

'I can't smell any sprouts,' he said, as he climbed out of the boat.

'That's because they've not been cooked,' Beatrix replied. 'Sprouts save up all their smell for when they're cooked.'

'Well, not all their smell,' Oi added. 'They save up some for after they've been eaten. But the less said about that the better. Let's pull the boat as far up the beach as we can and unload the supplies.'

Beatrix, Oi and Wilfred spent the rest of the day carrying the cases and boxes and barrels to the forest. (I say 'carried', but by this stage their arms were so heavy from all the rowing that they were dragging, pushing and shoving everything with shoulders, knees, feet and backs.) They found a small clearing in the woods to make camp and collected dry wood to make a fire.

'The captain was wrong about this island,' Beatrix said, looking about at all the plants and trees. 'He said the only thing that grows here is sprouts. I'll get a fire going, then let's see what we've got to eat. I don't know about you two, but I'm starving.'

'So am I,' Oi said. 'I'm starting with this one.' He levered open a chest that had *Biscuits* stamped across the top. Inside he was surprised to find silky material.

'They must be wrapped up,' he said. 'Very thoughtful – you don't want your biscuits getting broken when you're on a sea voyage. Not with all those storms.' He started to pull out the material and was surprised to find he was holding a very expensive-looking silk dress. He reached into the chest again, looking for biscuits, but he couldn't find any. There were more clothes – fine wool trousers, several pairs of very large underpants, an overcoat, silk socks and stockings and several rolls of material. The material had pictures of dragons and Wobblers and castles embroidered on it.

'Well, that's *not* what I was expecting. What have you got, Wilfred?'

Wilfred had opened one labelled *Ham*. But instead of ham, it was stuffed with jewellery, rolled up paintings and bottles of rum.

'Nothing we can eat,' he said, sounding glum.

Beatrix opened another case. 'More clothes in this one,' she said. 'Lots of silk too.'

They opened all the boxes and barrels, growing

more disappointed and more hungry with each one.

'No food!' Beatrix said. 'Just clothes and paintings and jewellery, lots of bags of gold coins and fine linen and silk. What are we meant to eat?!'

There was one case left, with *Crackers (Very Dry)* written on it. Wilfred snapped off the lid.

'Crackers,' he said, staring at the rows of grey-brown crackers. They looked about as appetising as a piece of cardboard. He took a bite out of one. 'Very dry.' He passed some to Oi and Beatrix.

'We'll have to go looking for sprouts,' Oi said miserably. 'Crackers and sprouts. The worst dinner ever.'

Beatrix looked around at the treasure they'd unloaded from the chests.

'I'd say McCannonball was most definitely a pirate. This must be everything he's stolen. Well, not everything. There were lots of chests and barrels left on the ship,' she said. 'He's going to be very angry when he finds out we've taken his treasure.'

11

The Great Fireball in the Sky

'**I** know I probably shouldn't say this,' Oi said as they sat round the fire after a dinner of sprout soup, fried sprouts, and crackers with a sprout dip. 'Because we did just escape from McCannonball, who was going to hand you over, dead or alive, to the Evil Army. And survive a dangerous storm. But what on earth are we going to do? I mean, we're in the middle of the Sea of Sinking Ships and General Burpintime is on his way to Beluga, most probably with your aunt Esmerelda. He's sworn to destroy everything, including your family and, well, I know you're a queen and everything, but I just don't see how we're going to get out of this one. Are you *sure* you don't have any magical powers? The **Curse of the Wobblers** definitely says you have magical powers.'

Beatrix looked up at the stars. She remembered how she used to look up at them with Wilfred and Uncle Ivan from the roof of her palace. She remembered how they'd looked up at them after they defeated the Evil Army, when Uncle Ivan had told her about her parents.

'... And I said I was sure I didn't have special powers, because if I did, I'd know about it. Do you have any of that marshmallow left?' Beatrix said.

'What marshmallow?' Oi replied, a little too quickly.

'The bits of marshmallow boat you stuffed in your pockets before we left Riddletown and have been secretly eating ever since.'

'Oh, *that* marshmallow,' Oi said innocently. He reached into his pocket, pulled out a piece and picked off the fluff. 'Here you go,' he said. 'Are you going to magically transform it into a giant marshmallow boat so we can sail away?'

Beatrix took it, stuck it onto the end of a twig and held it near the fire.

'No, I'm going to toast it and then I'm going to eat it. And I don't know how we're going to get out of this one.' Beatrix stared into the fire. 'If I had magical powers we could take off and fly to Beluga, like all these little sparks rising up that seem to dance in the night air.' Beatrix was silent for a moment. She took a bite of marshmallow, then said, 'I wonder why the sparks all rise upwards?'

'Oh, that's easy,' Wilfred replied in a sleepy voice. 'I learnt this in science lessons, many years ago. The little sparks that fly upwards are actually tiny fairies. The flames from the fire transform pieces of wood and bark into orange and red fire fairies who fly away towards the great fireball in the sky.'

'The great fireball in the sky... you mean the *sun*?' Beatrix said.

'Yes, the sun disappears at night because it goes out, then the fire fairies fly up and away from fires into the night sky, relight the sun and it rises again the next day.' Wilfred yawned and stretched. 'As with most science, there's a very simple explanation. I thought I'd taught you that already.'

Beatrix looked into the fire and then down at the ground.

'And look, once the little sparks move away from the hot fire they fall to the ground. See?'

She picked up a little black particle from the ground with her finger and thumb and it crumbled to dust.

Wilfred stared at the smudgy mark on her fingers.

'I hope you didn't just kill a fairy. We've had enough bad luck without killing fire fairies.'

'I thought you didn't believe in magic and fairies and all that stuff?' said Oi, feeling about in his pocket for some more marshmallow.

'I don't believe in magic,' Wilfred replied. 'But fairies aren't magic, they're a fact of life. Like toadstools or cobwebs or snowflakes or very dry crackers.'

'I haven't killed any fairies,' Beatrix said. 'If you watch closely, you'll see that the little sparks fly upwards in the hot air, then when they move away from the hot air, they sink back down. The fire's making them move, it's carrying all these little sparks on hot air. Look at your cape.'

Wilfred had hung his cape on a stick near the fire to dry and it kept billowing outwards.

'The hot air is lifting that too.'

Wilfred rubbed his eyes and stared at his cape.

'Are you sure? Sounds very strange. Fire fairies seem much more realistic to me – otherwise, who lights the sun so it can shine in the morning? It would be nice to fly away though, that's for sure,' he said.

Beatrix stared into the fire. *It* would *be nice to fly away*, she thought. *But it would take an awful lot of hot air to lift up a person.*

The next day they were woken by the gentle pitter-patter of rain. Oi was the first to wake up, then Dog, who was sleeping next to him. (That was the advantage of having a dog – he was like a hot-water bottle, a hot-water bottle with very bad breath.) Jeff opened one eye, looked around, then decided he was better off going back to sleep. They'd made beds and blankets from all the clothes and material from the ship, and they were surprisingly comfortable.

It took Oi a few moments to remember where he was, and by the time he had, he wished he hadn't. An island full of sprouts in the middle of the Sea of Sinking Ships.

He got up and tried to make a fire, but it didn't last long in the drizzly rain.

Wilfred was up next, he stretched his stiff limbs and tipped a little of the rum he'd found on the wood.

'Now try again,' he said to Oi. This time the flames jumped all over the wood.

'Woah!' said Beatrix, sitting up and rubbing her eyes. 'What's in the bottle? Magic fire water?'

'Sort of. It's the captain's rum. It tastes terrible but it **burns** very well. I used rum when I learnt how to breathe fire.'

'You can breathe fire?' Oi said.

'Of course,' Wilfred replied. 'Watch…' He took a burning stick from the fire and a mouthful of rum, then he turned and sprayed the rum between his lips over the flame. It looked like a ball of flame had exploded from his mouth. Wilfred wiped his face. 'Mmm, doesn't taste too bad actually. Although it is a bit early in the morning for rum.'

Beatrix and Oi stared in amazement.

'Wow!' Beatrix said. 'We should have disguised you as the Riddletown Dragon. You could have burned General Burpintime to a crisp!'

She looked into the fire, thinking about the way she'd seen Wilfred's coat billow outwards because of the hot air. She had an idea, or at least the beginnings of one.

'Hold the other side of this piece of silk would you?' she said.

Wilfred frowned. 'What are we doing, folding it up?'

'No, I want to try something. Let's stand either side of the fire. Don't hold the silk too close to the flames, I don't want it to burn. I want to see if it lifts up.'

The two of them held the material above the flames.

'Look!' Beatrix said. 'See the middle of the silk? It's pulling upwards. You can *feel* it.'

'So it is,' said Wilfred. He loosened his grip slightly on the silk and it billowed upwards. 'Perhaps the fire fairies are pushing it towards the sun.'

'I don't think so,' Beatrix said. 'It's the hot air from the fire. If we could catch all that hot air in an enormous bag, somehow hold on to that bag as it lifts up, then maybe we could get away from this island and fly to Beluga.'

Wilfred and Oi were silent for a moment.

Then Oi said: 'That sounds like the maddest thing I've ever heard. I love it! It would be like a giant ball, but open at one end so you could fill it with hot air.'

'It's *craziness*,' said Wilfred. 'And far too dangerous. Only a lunatic would attempt something so crazy.'

'A ball-lunatic,' Oi said. 'That's what we could call it. A ballunatic.'

'Or a ball*oon*,' Beatrix said.

'A balloon of doom,' Wilfred said, gloomily.

'Even if we could build it, we'll end up falling into the sea. We couldn't hold on for long enough to get to Beluga.'

'Then let's tie the balloon to something,' said Beatrix. 'A little boat. A basket. Something light and strong we can sit in. Wilfred – you can do your fire-breathing trick if we ever start to sink. All we'd need is a strong easterly wind. Have you got any better ideas?'

Wilfred frowned. 'We could try and capture the fire fairies, tie tiny pieces of thread to them and train them to lift us up?' he said after a pause.

'I prefer Beatrix's idea,' Oi said.

And so it was that the world's first hot-air balloon was invented on an island in the middle of the Sea of Sinking Ships by a ten-year-old girl many hundreds of years ago. If you're wondering why you've never heard of this, it's because there weren't any historians to write it down. Beatrix used charcoal to draw her design on a large rock. She decided the balloon would have to be as big as they could possibly make it, and the basket to hold them would need to be as light as possible. She drew something that would look to you or me like a light bulb, although of course light bulbs hadn't been invented yet either.

Beatrix knew it was risky. How long would the hot air last? What if the wind changed direction? Would birds try and attack it? How cold was the sea? Where would you go to the loo? But she tried not to think about the dangers. She left that to Wilfred – he was much better at worrying than her.

12

How to Make a
Hot-air Balloon

It's very simple to explain how to make a hot-air
balloon. Firstly, you make a balloon. Then you
attach it to a basket. Then you fill it with hot air,
and *away you go*. But it's also very simple to describe
how to build a house. Firstly, you get some bricks.
Then you stick them together. Then you add a roof.
The making of things is usually a lot harder than
the explaining of things. Even making a basket is a
lot harder than you might think.

The rain had stopped but the wind was blowing and it was difficult to lay out all the different pieces of material across the beach without them flapping about.

'Right,' Beatrix said, using stones to hold down the various pairs of pants and pieces of silk and stockings. 'We'll use a bent nail and thread to stitch them together. Wilfred, you can start work on the basket. Oh, and stop drinking that rum!'

Wilfred put the bottle down. 'I wasn't drinking it – I was practising holding it in my mouth, ready for some more fire breathing.' He took another sip and swallowed. 'You see the difference?'

Wilfred walked up the beach and into the woods. He was looking for strong but thin branches. Most of the trees were tall and looked very old indeed, but there were younger saplings growing between them that would bend and could be woven together. He cut some down, then followed the path deeper into the woods. He was going uphill now, towards the centre of the island.

He stopped for a rest once he'd gone halfway up the hill, and gazed out to sea, wondering if Beatrix's idea to make a giant ballunatic was madness or genius. He hoped the fire fairies would be on their side. He hated to think of them all trapped inside it, unable to fly to the sun.

As he laid out the saplings he'd cut he saw something on the horizon. *Was it a ship?* He blinked and stared for a moment. It was hard to tell if the

light was playing tricks on him. *Yes, that's exactly what it was.* The longer he looked at it the bigger it got. He could make out the sails, white against the grey sky. There was a good wind behind it and it was cutting nicely through the waves.

For a moment he was filled with *relief.* Someone must have seen the smoke from their fire and decided to come and rescue them! He was about to run and tell Beatrix the good news when he paused and had another look at the ship.

There was something very familiar about it. It was still a long way off, but he was sure it had a wonky mast at the front that looked like it had been damaged in a storm. Wilfred's feeling of relief and excitement turned to something else. Captain McCannonball!

Wilfred picked up the pile of sticks and branches and ran as fast as he could back to the beach. Time for some *extremely fast* basket weaving!

13

The Evil Avalanche

That same day, early in the morning, General Burpintime had awoken, feeling even more grumpy than usual. Firstly, he'd run out of marshmallows, so he couldn't have any with his breakfast. Porridge without marshmallows simply wasn't the same. It tasted like – well, it tasted like *porridge*. Secondly, they'd used up all their wood to make horse skis, so no one could build him a nice warm fire. Thirdly, because there was no nice warm fire, he couldn't melt the snow, which meant he couldn't have a nice warm bath.

General Burpintime liked to start each day with a nice warm bath, followed by a bowl of porridge with melted marshmallows. Deelicious. But there was no bath and there were no marshmallows, and if that wasn't bad enough, it had turned out that horse skis weren't actually a bad idea. In fact, they were a very good idea, and Esmerelda wouldn't let him forget it. They'd made it through the mountains in no time at all, sliding through villages, flattening anything that got in their way, from houses to fences to snowmen children had spent hours building. The Evil Army had become the Evil Avalanche, and this pleased him greatly. Or at least it would have pleased him greatly, if horse skis had been his invention. Because they were Esmerelda's invention, it annoyed him enormously.

When the stories of his adventures were written, he decided he'd change that bit, so that it was him on the mountain, staring heroically into the distance, and coming up with the brilliant idea of horse skis.

The book would be called something like **General Burpintime the Brilliant**. No need to mention Esmerelda. And if he did mention her, she

would be saying how clever he was. He drew a little sketch in his notebook of a horse on skis, then he started to get dressed, taking off his pyjamas and putting on an enormous pair of Evil Army underpants. It wouldn't take much longer to get to Beluga, probably only a day or two. Then they would hide outside the castle and wait for Esmerelda to carry out her plan.

He dipped a piece of wool in honey and popped it in his mouth. It wasn't as good as a marshmallow, but it was the closest thing he had.

'What on earth are you eating? And why haven't you packed? We're about to set off.'

Burpintime jumped and spat out the sticky wool. How did Esmerelda manage to creep up on him without his noticing? He decided tents would be much better if they had a door you had to knock on. Then again, that didn't stop Esmerelda either.

'What do you mean you're *about* to set off?' he said.

'I mean I've already ordered the soldiers to pack their things away, steal whatever food they want from the surrounding villages and get ready to march to Beluga.'

'You can't do that! I'm the General – I tell them what to do!'

'Oh, don't be such a ninny,' Esmerelda said. 'We need to get a move on. We can't hang around while you draw things in your little book.' She pointed at the notebook on General Burpintime's bed. 'What's that drawing? It looks like a stick horse on skis.'

'None of your business.' General Burpintime grabbed the book off the bed. He was going to put it in his trouser pocket, then he realised he hadn't had time to put his trousers on yet and was still in his enormous Evil Army underpants.

Just then, two soldiers entered the tent and started to pack away all General Burpintime's things – his super comfy pillow, the medals he placed by his bed each night when he went to sleep, and his three spare uniforms he always took with him in case one of them got dirty.

'What are you doing?' he said.

'Packing,' they said.

They began to roll up the sides of the tent too, and take apart the frame. General Burpintime realised he was standing in the middle of a field full of soldiers without any trousers on.

'Stop it! Wait! I didn't tell you to pack anything away. I'm not ready yet!' he shouted.

All the soldiers in the field around him stopped what they were doing and turned and stared. Even the horses turned and stared.

'What are you looking at? Get on with being an Evil Army,' he said, before hastily pulling on his trousers. 'This is all your fault, Esmerelda,' he said. 'I've never been so embarrassed in my life!'

'Really?' Esmerelda replied. 'What about the time that dog pushed you over into the muddy water of the River Riddle, and tore off your dragon head whilst Beatrix the Bold floated away with all the children you'd taken prisoner?'

General Burpintime made a '*Hhhhhmmmmmmmpppphhhh!*' sort of noise and pulled out a piece of wool that had got stuck between his teeth.

'It can't be good for you, chewing wool like that,' she said. 'It'll ruin your teeth. Now, are you ready to go?'

General Burpintime looked around. His soldiers were standing in neat rows, his tent had been packed. One of his soldiers placed his fur coat gently over his shoulders. He had to admit, it all looked very well organised. He pulled on his trousers.

'Onward march!' Esmerelda shouted, while General Burpintime was still putting on his boots. Ten thousand soldiers stepped forward as one.

'Halt! Stop! No marching!' General Burpintime said. 'I give the orders around here.'

The soldiers stopped marching, bumping into one another.

'Go on then,' Esmerelda said.

'I will, thank you very much. ONWARD MARCH!' General Burpintime shouted at the top of his voice.

The soldiers didn't move. They looked at Esmerelda, as if they were seeking permission. She nodded her head, a tiny movement. The soldiers started marching. General Burpintime didn't notice.

'That's more like it,' he said. 'Now, where are we going?'

Esmerelda climbed up on her horse (which was no longer wearing skis, and was very happy about that). 'This way,' she said.

14

Lift Off!

'They're coming – they're coming!' Wilfred shouted. 'McCannonball is on his way!' He threw the bundle of sticks on the ground.

The *Cutty Shark* was no longer a dot on the horizon. Like the cannon ball in Oi's favourite cannonball joke, it was getting bigger and bigger, and was soon going to hit Devil Sprout Island.

Beatrix and Oi looked up. They'd been so busy

cutting and stitching the material to make the balloon that they hadn't noticed the ship bearing down on the island.

'Oi, you help Wilfred make a basket. I'm going to dig out a fire pit – the balloon's ready,' Beatrix said.

'Will do,' Oi said. 'Although I'm not sure how much I can remember about basket weaving. I only completed Grade One when I was at school.'

'I got a Merit for Grade Three,' Wilfred said.

'If I remember rightly, we start by splitting the branch in the middle and pushing the other ones through, then we bend those branches up to make the sides and weave the others around them.'

Oi and Wilfred set to work, wishing they'd paid more attention in basket-weaving lessons. They worked as fast as they could, and it wasn't long before they had something resembling a rather messy nest.

'It's not going to be the best-looking basket, but it feels sturdy. How long before the fire's ready?' said Wilfred.

Beatrix climbed into the pit. 'I'll light it now and I can start filling the balloon while you finish off the basket.'

The pit she'd dug for the fire was slightly smaller than the bottom of the balloon, and nice and deep, so they could put the base of the balloon over it and catch all the hot air without burning the material.

Beatrix poured rum onto the wood, then made sparks with her fire stone and piece of metal, setting the kindling alight. She blew into the flames to help them on their way, then climbed quickly out of the pit. *Very* quickly.

'Time to get the balloon in place,' she said, dragging it across the beach and pulling the base so it was over the fire pit, ready to catch the hot air. She attached ropes to hold it down and tied them round stones, then she stood back and watched. And waited. And watched. And waited some more.

'Could take a while to fill up,' Oi said, looking anxiously at Captain McCannonball's ship. 'The basket's ready. How long do you think we have?'

'I don't know.' Beatrix shrugged. 'Not much we can do though.'

Then the base of the balloon started to puff outwards. The long flat shape was, very slowly, lifting up off the beach. It was like watching a cake rise in its tin.

In the distance they heard a loud bang, then the whistle of something flying through the air. All three of them ducked instinctively. It crashed into the woods, splintering tree trunks.

'What was that?' Oi said.

'McCannonball,' Beatrix replied. 'He's firing at us!'

'McCannonball's cannonballs!' Wilfred exclaimed as another crashed into the sea, sending a spray of saltwater towards them.

The balloon had lifted up off the beach and was at last beginning to strain at the ropes holding it down. It looked like a giant, multi-coloured cloud, keen to take off and join the others in the sky.

BOOM!

Another cannonball sailed past them – this one only just missed the balloon.

'We need to attach the basket! Quick, help me with the rigging.' Beatrix looped ropes round the basket so it was tied to the bottom of the balloon, then dropped Dog and Jeff into it. Wilfred collected together the last few bottles of rum, just in case he needed to breathe fire up into the balloon during their flight.

'Good job we didn't bring Jeff the horse,' Oi said. 'I don't think he'd have fit in.'

BOOM. The next cannonball crashed into the beach, sending stones flying towards them.

'His aim's getting better!' Beatrix said. 'Wilfred, you get in – Oi and I will cut through the ropes.'

Wilfred dived into the basket. Beatrix cut through two of the ropes then jumped over the side, but as Oi was cutting through the last rope a sudden gust of wind caught hold of the balloon, and it shot upwards.

'Nooooooo!' Beatrix shouted.

Oi felt the rope pull away from him. He dropped his knife and grabbed hold of it, gripping tightly as the balloon surged upwards with an almighty whoosh. He clung desperately on, the balloon rising higher and higher above the island.

Beatrix and Wilfred reached down to help him, while Dog barked and tried to climb up the sides of the basket.

'Here! Grab my hand,' Beatrix said.

Oi stretched upwards, holding on with one arm and gripping the rope with his legs. He was being blown all over the place. It was like trying to climb an angry snake.

'Here!' Beatrix said, and with Wilfred's help she heaved Oi over the side.

'Phew.' Oi took deep breaths and slumped down in the basket.

'Are you all right?' Beatrix said. 'Your face is *very* green.'

'I'm OK. Just a bit sick from getting blown about. In fact I might just...' He stood up again and leant over the side.

Beatrix and Wilfred looked in the other direction. They were extremely relieved to see Oi in the basket but they didn't want to see his lunch again too. They heard a gurgling sound that turned into a burp, one of those long burps that means something else might be coming up, like the whistle of a train before it comes hurtling out of the tunnel. '*UrrrrrgggggguurrgggggghhhhuuuhHHHHH!*'

Oi reached into his pocket for a handkerchief. 'Better out than in,' he said, wiping his mouth with it.

Far below, Captain McCannonball was staring upwards and shaking his fist at the giant flying clothes-ball. He wasn't sure what sort of magic this Beatrix girl had used to make all the fine clothes he'd stolen fly away, but whatever it was it made him VERY ANGRY.

As he stared upwards, he could see something else, something that looked like a big green cloud. He'd never seen a big green cloud. Grey ones, white ones, even ones that looked a bit purple, or a bit pink – but never a green one. He'd also never seen a cloud fall out of the sky, but that's exactly what this one seemed to be doing. It was falling towards him, and it was getting bigger and bigger and bigger as it fell.

Three seconds later, the green cloud hit him, splattering all over his fine clothes and hair and his carefully combed moustache. The captain pulled out a handkerchief and wiped the disgusting green slime off his face. A *sprout cloud?!* he thought.

Beatrix, Oi and Wilfred held on tightly to the sides of the basket as it flew high over the sea. Beatrix had the same feeling she'd had when she'd stood on the roof of her palace and looked out for the first time at the world around her. She felt exhilarated and alive. Even Oi was starting to get used to the strange sensation of moving through the air.

They kept an eye out for any sign of land. They didn't know exactly where they were going, but at last Beatrix felt as if she was on her way home;

she'd get to Beluga in time to warn her parents about General Burpintime and Esmerelda.

'You two have a rest first,' Wilfred said. 'I'll keep watch. I can always do my fire breathing trick if we start to sink.'

Beatrix and Oi crouched down in the basket, huddled together with Dog and Jeff to try to keep warm. Wilfred kept watch, his eyes fixed on the dim line where the grey sea merged with the darkening sky.

For the first half hour, he managed to stay awake. Occasionally he took a sip of rum and blew flames up into the balloon. Occasionally he took a sip of rum and simply swallowed it. For the next half hour, he could feel his eyelids grow heavy, he had to keep humming to himself to stay awake and he didn't do as much fire breathing. After that, his head nodded forward gently, so he thought it would be wise to rest it on his hands.

After that, well, after that he dropped gently backwards into the basket and fell sound asleep. He didn't notice that the wind had changed direction, and was now blowing them southwards. Even if he had noticed it, it wouldn't have mattered – it wasn't as if he could do anything about it. You can't change the way the wind blows.

15

Where Are We?

Waking up in the basket of a hot-air balloon is a **very strange** sensation. Even stranger than waking up in a pile of stolen clothes on an island in the Sea of Sinking Ships.

Beatrix was the first to wake. It was still the middle of the night but she could hear a soft, scraping sound, as if someone was brushing the floor of the basket. She rubbed her eyes. That didn't make sense. There was hardly any floor to brush, they hadn't brought a broom and anyway she'd never seen Oi nor Wilfred do any sweeping. She heard the scraping sound again. It was coming from underneath the basket. She was certain water wouldn't make that noise.

'Oi, Wilfred, wake up! Can you hear that?' she said. She stood up, holding onto the sides of the basket and looking down. It was hard to see, but she could just make out that whatever was beneath them moved like waves, but somehow wasn't.

Wilfred and Oi looked around.

They all heard the brushing sound again.

All three looked at one another.

'TREES!' they said together. The basket sank even lower, brushing the tree tops.

'Wilfred, *quick*, we need fire to lift us up or we're going to crash!' Beatrix said.

Wilfred felt his pockets: fire stone and piece of metal to make a spark, dry grass to catch the spark and start the fire, rag soaked in rum and tied to

a stick to light, all ready to start fire breathing...

CRUUUUUNNNNCCHHHHHHH!

They were thrown to one side of the basket. The balloon was no longer flying. The basket was stuck in a tree top. The half-empty balloon flapped above them, still trying to lift them up but without the same enthusiasm as it had when it was filled to bursting with hot air.

'The fire fairies have all flown away!' Wilfred exclaimed.

'Are we there?' Oi said hopefully.

'No. Beluga is a large town on the coast off the Sea of Sinking Ships, with an enormous castle in the middle of it. As you can see from all these trees, we're in a forest,' Beatrix said.

'Where are we then?' Oi said.

'That is a good question,' Wilfred replied. 'We were definitely going in the right direction when we left the island, and I'm pretty sure we're not back on the island. I can't see the sea. So we must be inland. It's possible that the wind changed direction and blew us off course.'

'I'd say it was more than possible,' Beatrix replied. 'And from what I remember of the map, the forest on the way to my parents' castle is…' She paused. She didn't want to say what she was thinking.

'**Wobbler Woods**?!' Oi said. 'Please don't tell me we've been blown all the way back to

Wobbler Woods! That means we're even further away than when we left Riddletown!'

'And we're in a wood full of Wobblers,' Wilfred said. 'Which fortunately do not exist, otherwise we'd be in real trouble.'

As soon as he'd said it, they heard a bone-chilling, blood-curdling, spine-tingling *Hooooowwwwwllll*.

'I'd say we were in real trouble anyway,' Beatrix said. 'We're stuck up a tree in the middle of the night in a forest that seems to be home to howling wolves.'

The basket lurched to one side as one of the branches it was resting on cracked. A flock of birds awoke and took flight, their wings flapping noisily.

Beatrix, Oi and Wilfred held onto the sides, waiting to see if they'd fall further. They didn't. The basket was pinned in place by the tree's branches.

'Well, Jeff,' Beatrix said, opening up his cage and taking him out carefully, 'I think it might be time for you to go and get help.'

Jeff opened one eye, gave what seemed to be a little shrug, then closed his eye again.

'I don't think he's going anywhere till morning,' Oi said.

'Oi's right. Pigeons aren't nocturnal. We should have brought an owl too, in case we needed to send a message at night,' Wilfred said.

'Also, how can you use Jeff to tell Uncle Ivan where we are if we don't know where we are?' Oi said.

Beatrix put Jeff back in the cage and rubbed her eyes. It had been a long day. And a long night. And the night wasn't even over.

'I thought he could just bring Uncle Ivan back here,' Beatrix replied.

'I'm not sure that's how a homing pigeon works,' Wilfred said. 'I think they only go in one direction, home. I don't think he can show Uncle Ivan the way back. A rescue dog could, but not a homing pigeon.'

Then they all looked at Dog. He looked back at them as if to say *Seriously?*

'As much as we all love Dog and his brilliant dragon-slaying skills, I don't think he's going to be able to find his way back to the palace and bring Uncle Ivan here. Also, there are wolves out there. It's too dangerous,' Beatrix said. 'It'll have to be Jeff. I'll write a note on a sliver of bark and tie it to his leg.'

'What are you going to say?'

'I'm going to say that we're in Wobbler Woods, not far from the coast. They'll know where we are because there's a great big balloon flapping about above the trees. If they see that, then they'll find us just beneath it.'

Beatrix used her knife to scrape the message into a tiny piece of bark.

Wobbler Woods. Tree with balloon. Help. B.

She made a hole in it, looped a thin piece of material through and tied it to one of Jeff's legs.

'Well, my little bird, Uncle Ivan says you're the best he's got, so let's see you fly home.' She lifted Jeff up and launched him forwards. Jeff's eyes

opened suddenly, his wings flapped in a confused sort of way and he landed on a nearby branch.

'Go!' Beatrix said. 'Fly home!'

Jeff looked around, nestled his head under his wing, then went back to sleep.

Beatrix sat down in the basket. No one said anything. No one could think of what to say.

They'd run out of ideas. They'd run out of pigeons. Well, they only had one to begin with, but you know what I mean.

Wilfred scratched his head. As a grown-up, he thought it was his job to try and cheer Oi and Beatrix up, but for once he couldn't think of anything at all to say.

'I'm sure things will look better in the morning,' he said at last. 'They usually do.'

A wolf howled hungrily, somewhere below them. It sounded closer this time.

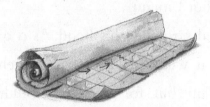

16

Wobbler Woods

They didn't manage to get much sleep in the rickety basket, high in the trees with the wolves circling below them, but when morning came Wilfred was proved right. Things didn't look so bad. Not if you kept your gaze on the tree tops and didn't look down.

From their high position, they could see for miles. Far away to the east, through the early morning mist, they could make out the towers of Uncle Ivan's palace. They rose in disorderly splendour, up into the sky.

It was disappointing to realise how far back the wind must have blown them, but they were pleased to see a familiar sight. It meant they weren't lost. To the south they could see a deep blue line on the horizon – the Sea of Sinking Ships – to the north was the grey outline of Riddletown and, to the west, a long, long way away, was the city of Beluga.

'You see?' Wilfred said. 'At least we know where we are.'

Jeff had woken too, and was tottering about on his branch.

'Fly, Jeff! Fly home!' Beatrix said. 'That way!' She pointed towards the palace.

Jeff did one of his funny little shrugs, then took off. He flew

 towards Beluga, then seemed to change his mind, turned around and started flying out towards the Sea of Sinking Ships. Then he changed his mind again, circled the balloon, which was still flapping about in the wind, and flew towards the palace. Then he changed his mind and settled down on another branch.

'Home, Jeff!' they all shouted. 'Home!'

Jeff looked up as if he'd just remembered something, then flew off towards the palace.

'I think he's got it!' Oi said. 'He'll be back there in no time. And Ivan the Vicious should be able to get here in a couple of days. He can clear a path through the woods with his army.'

Beatrix turned and looked towards Beluga.

'We're not going to get to Beluga before the Evil Army, are we?' she said.

'I'm afraid not,' Wilfred replied. 'But when we

get there, we'll have your uncle's army.'

'And there'll be a battle,' Oi said. 'A tremendous battle. Which we'll win, of course.'

'How?' Beatrix said after a pause.

'How what?' Oi replied.

'How will we win the battle?' Beatrix said.

Oi was silent for a moment. He was about to say *I'm sure you'll think of something* – when a loud, shouty voice interrupted him.

'ARE YOU GOING TO STAY UP THERE ALL DAY OR DO YOU WANT TO COME DOWN AND HAVE SOME BREAKFAST?!'

Beatrix, Oi and Wilfred peered over the side. They couldn't see who was at the bottom of the tree because of all the pine needles.

'Do you think it's a trap?' Oi said. 'Whoever it is wants to lure us down with promises of breakfast, then murder us and steal Dog.'

'IT'S NOT A TRAP!' said the voice.

'Well, it looks like it's not a trap,' Beatrix said.

'That's what they'd say if it was a trap!' Oi said.

'AND IT'S ALSO WHAT WE'D SAY IF IT WASN'T A TRAP! COME ON DOWN, WE'VE GOT FRESH FARTINPANTS.'

'Who are you?' Beatrix said.

'WOBBLERS!' came the reply. 'You're in Wobbler Woods.'

'Wobblers?!' Beatrix replied.

'Wobblers!' Wilfred repeated.

'Are you sure?' shouted Oi.

'OF COURSE WE'RE SURE!' the Wobblers shouted back.

'Come on, Oi and Wilfred,' Beatrix said. She'd heard many stories about Wobblers – from the fact that they hid in the forest and ate small children, to them losing their third eye at the age of seven – but she'd never heard anything about them having fartinpants for breakfast.

She climbed over the side of the basket, feeling

for a branch that was strong enough to take her weight, then made her way down carefully, pushing the prickly pine needles out of her way. Oi followed, holding onto Dog with one arm while he made his way down. Wilfred decided he didn't want to be alone in the basket at the top of the tree, so he began his climb too.

17

Peter the Wobbler

It was much darker on the ground than it was in the tree tops, because the branches blocked out the light. In the gloom, Beatrix could make out four strange shapes, half-animal, half-human, half-mud.

Hang on, she thought. *That's not right*. OK – half-animal, half-human and covered in mud and leaves and twigs. You couldn't have three halves. Or maybe you could, if you were a **Wobbler**!

They held spears and wore clothes made from animal skins and old pieces of material. They were standing very still.

'I'm Peter,' the tallest of the four Wobblers said.

'Peter the Wobbler?' Beatrix replied. She thought it was a strange name for a mythical beast. And anyway, Wobblers didn't exist.

'Yes. And this is Freya, this is Bronwin and last of all we have Erick.' Peter spoke in a very serious

voice, as if being a Wobbler was a very serious business. He was so serious that Beatrix had to fight the urge to smile.

 'I'm Beatrix the Bold,' she said, feeling rather surprised that **Wobblers**, which she knew didn't exist, were now standing right in front of her saying they did exist. 'I'm Queen of Beluga, so I suppose, according to the curse, you're the army who's going to help me defeat General Burpintime. I was rather hoping there might be a few more of you –'

Beatrix was interrupted by the sound of wood splitting, then a thump as Oi hit the ground.

'Morning, I'm Oi. Where are those fartinpants?'

Before anyone could answer, they heard the sound of more branches breaking, and another thump on the other side of the tree. Wilfred got up stiffly, rubbing his knee.

'Ouch. It's a long time since I climbed a tree. Especially one that tall.'

'Wilfred and Oi, I'd like to introduce you to Peter, Freya, Bronwin and Erick,' Beatrix said.

Wilfred blinked and rubbed his eyes.

'Peter the Wobbler?' he said, grinning.

'Yes,' Peter replied. 'What's so funny about that?'

'Nothing, nothing at all. It's just that Wobblers don't exist.'

The four Wobblers held up their spears, spun them round, threw them in the air, turned a circle, caught the spears, performed a backflip with the spear stuck in the ground, then crouched down. They scraped the point of their spears on the earth in front of them, drawing a semi-circle. A perfectly executed battle dance, a ninja ballet, with added weapons. When they finished they shouted '*Hiiiiyah!*'

'That was a very Wobblery thing to do,' Oi said, looking both surprised and impressed. 'Perhaps

you do exist. Now, about those fartinpants. I really am rather hungry.'

Peter had a leather bag slung over his shoulder. He opened it and took out the flat cakes, passing them round.

'So,' Peter said. 'You're Beatrix the Bold?'

'That's right,' Beatrix replied, between mouthfuls.

'What are you doing in Wobbler Woods, and how on earth did you get to the top of that tree?'

'Long story,' Beatrix said. 'We were on our way to Beluga.'

'By ballunatic,' Wilfred said.

'By *balloon*,' Oi explained.

'What's a balloon?' said Erick. He was the smallest of the Wobblers, but he had a very deep voice.

'It's that thing flapping about above the trees. Fill it with hot air and it floats. Like a ship, only it floats through air, not water,' Beatrix said. 'And it's much harder to make it go in one direction.

Which is why we ended up going in the wrong direction.'

'Why didn't you just go by ship to Beluga?' Peter asked. 'It would only take a few days.'

'We did, but we ran into some trouble. Turned out the captain of the ship was a pirate who wanted to sell me to the Evil Army.'

'Was it Captain McCannonball?'

'It was! Have you heard of him?'

Peter nodded. 'You were lucky to get away. He has a ship full of treasures he's stolen. Most of his passengers are never seen again.'

Beatrix nodded grimly, then asked, 'How many of you are there? I'm guessing there are more than four.'

'There are fifteen of us,' Freya said.

'Fifteen?' Wilfred said. 'That's not exactly an army. I think General Burpintime has about ten thousand soldiers.'

Beatrix looked at the four Wobblers. She was

still trying to work out how these four children had turned themselves into Wobblers.

'So how exactly did you become Wobblers? Don't you miss your families?'

Peter frowned. 'Of course,' he said. 'But we'll see them again one day, and in the meantime we get to be Wobblers and terrify soldiers from the Evil Army whenever they come into our woods.'

Wilfred brushed the crumbs off his cape. It was starting to look a little scruffy now, and had torn when he fell through the last few branches of the tree. 'So let me get this straight,' he said. 'You really are Wobblers?'

'We really are Wobblers,' Freya said.

'That means Wobblers *do* exist!' said Oi, turning to Beatrix. 'You told me they didn't.'

'The ones in the stories don't exist,' said Beatrix. 'The ones that gobble up children and look like weasels crossed with goblins don't exist, but these ones do. Look, they're right in front of you.'

'So does that mean the curse is true?' Oi said, scratching his head.

Beatrix frowned, then smiled. 'It means it *can* come true. If we defeat the Evil Army with the help of the Wobblers and chase them from their lands, I suppose it will have come true.'

'Even if you didn't believe in it?' Oi said.

'I don't think it matters if I believe in it or not,' Beatrix said. 'What matters is whether the Evil Army believes in it. If they think an army of Wobblers is going to defeat them because of a curse, then they're going to be terrified when they see an army of Wobblers approaching.'

'But what if there *are* only fifteen Wobblers in that army?' Oi said. 'What do you think, Peter – are you up for fighting ten thousand very angry soldiers?'

Peter picked up his spear and threw it into the tree a few centimetres above Oi's head.

'No problem,' he said. 'I'm up for fighting anything!'

'Including a tree, by the looks of it,' Oi said, as he got up and pulled the spear out of the tree trunk.

18

Uncle Ivan Gets the Message

Although it had only been a week and a half since Beatrix left the palace at the end of Numb Butt Lane, it felt an awful lot longer to Ivan the Vicious. The palace seemed a lot less bright without her, and it was quieter too, which he thought he'd like, but found he didn't really like.

He decided to check the falconry again to see if Jeff had returned. He'd already checked it twice that morning, but he didn't like the thought of missing him. The falconry was high up in the palace and as he stood looking out for Jeff he could see for miles – all the way to the snow-capped mountains in the distance.

He stared at them, wondering where Beatrix was, hoping she was safe. He was about to go when he noticed a bird circling high in the sky. It looked a bit confused, as if it wasn't sure whether it had the right palace. It swooped down to get a closer look then flew away again. Finally it dived down towards him and landed neatly on the palace wall.

Uncle Ivan looked at it. Then looked at it again.

'Jeff?' he said.

Jeff didn't respond. But then Jeff didn't ever respond to anything. He was a pigeon, after all.

Ivan reached out slowly. 'Here, Jeff.' He held out his hand, his forefinger outstretched.

Jeff flapped his wings, jumped up and then perched on his finger. Ivan gently removed the

sliver of bark that was tied to Jeff's leg. He read the tiny message scratched into the surface:

Wobbler Woods. Tree with balloon. Help. B.

Balloon? Ivan thought. *What's a balloon? Some sort of ball, maybe?*

He looked towards Wobbler Woods. He could see something in the distance, at least a day's ride away. Something flapping in the wind, as if it was a kite caught in a tree.

No kite could be that big. It must be the size of a ship's sail – a huge sail, made up of all sorts of colours. He ran back inside, down the winding staircase, along the twisting corridors.

'Mrs Fartinpants! Quick! I must get ready. I need a horse. And some fartinpants, lots of fartinpants. Jeff is back. He has a message from Beatrix. She's in Wobbler Woods. How can she only be in Wobbler Woods? She should be in Beluga by now. I'm worried something terrible has happened!'

'I'll come with you,' Mrs Fartinpants said. 'I don't want any **Wobblers** getting their hands on my Beatrix! No time to make fartinpants,' she said, 'but I'll bring the ingredients with me, just in case.'

She threw a frying pan, some eggs and a bag of flour into a bag, ran to the stables and jumped up onto a horse, quick as a flash.

'What are you waiting for, Ivan?' she called over her shoulder, ready to gallop out of the gates.

Ivan stared after her in astonishment. That was definitely the fastest fartinpant he'd ever seen.

19

Talking Trees and Horse-cows

It was early evening and the winter sun was setting behind the walled city of Beluga. On one side of the city was the Sea of Sinking Ships and on the other side was a forest. If you'd been walking in the forest that particular night as the sun was going down, you'd have seen some *very* strange things.

For a start, a lot of the trees looked decidedly odd, most untree-like, in fact. These trees weren't like the tall oak trees and the fir trees that reached towards the darkening sky. They were much shorter, with only one or two branches. They were also extremely angry-looking, which I think you'll agree is very strange for a tree. You get sad trees, like a weeping willow, you can even get confused trees, like a monkey puzzle tree, but you don't tend to get angry trees.

As well as the angry-looking trees, there was a large number of cows. What's unusual about a cow? There's nothing unusual about a cow, but you don't tend to find hundreds of cows wandering about in a forest at night. These cows had long necks and were very horse-like. In fact, if you looked closely, you'd have found

that some of them still had splodges of black and white paint on them.

The horses were not very happy about this, and neither were the trees, but General Burpintime had insisted they wear disguises, given how close they were to Beluga. Esmerelda had argued with him about that, as she argued with him about everything. At the moment, she was arguing with him about the best way to get an army of ten thousand soldiers into a castle with very thick walls that also had ten thousand soldiers inside it.

'I've been thinking about your plan,' General Burpintime said through the branches that covered most of his face. 'I don't like it any more. I think we should make a battering ram, then smash that through the gates – that's the sensible option. The traditional Evil Army approach. Chop down, smash through, destroy. I can direct the soldiers from somewhere nice and safe. Simple, but effective. I doubt your sister will even let you in.'

'Of course she will. She trusts me.'

'I don't trust you. Why would your sister trust you?'

'Because she is a trusting person. You aren't.'

'How long will it take for you to open the castle gates?'

'I don't know. An hour or two?' Esmerelda said. 'I'll have to convince my sister I'm being chased by the Evil Army. I'll have to make up a story about you taking over my palace and Ivan hiding somewhere with Beatrix. While I'm doing that, you need to get as close as you can to the castle.' She frowned and paused. 'Then I'll throw a flaming torch from the tower above the gates. That'll be the signal for you and your army to walk straight in and attack. No need for a battering ram.'

General Burpintime wanted to disagree. That's because he really wanted to make a battering ram. He wanted to say Esmerelda's plan didn't make sense and his plan was much better – but it wasn't. And he knew it. He huffed and he puffed and then he told Esmerelda to hurry up and get on with it.

Later that night, Esmerelda stood outside the city gates of Beluga, a friendly smile fixed on her face. A smile she had been practising for the last few days. A smile that said, *Oh, how lovely it is to see you, a ha ha ha.* A smile that didn't say, *Oh, how much I'd like to kill you all and steal your gold.*

She had told the guards she wanted to see her sister. She had important news: the Evil Army were going to try and take over Beluga and she had made a very dangerous journey in order to warn them.

At last she heard footsteps and her sister's annoyingly sweet voice telling the guards to open the city gates. A moment later the huge gates swung open, and there she was. Isabella the Intelligent.

She wore a magnificent dressing gown made from golden thread and an enormous golden crown on her head. The crown looked a bit wobbly

and there were two servants standing either side of her, ready to catch it if it toppled off.

Esmerelda felt two things when she saw her sister. She felt the tiniest bit guilty about what she was planning to do, and she also felt jealous. She felt a lot more jealous than she felt guilty, especially when she looked at Isabella's magnificent and extremely fancy dressing gown and her enormous golden crown. Esmerelda had been trekking (and sliding) through the mountains for several days. She looked more like a Wobbler than a princess or a queen. There were twigs stuck in her hair, her dress was torn and tatty and she hadn't had a bath for at least two weeks. Isabella, on the other hand, looked like she'd got dressed up just to go to bed.

'Esmerelda, my dear sister! Is everything all right?' Isabella said, her face a picture of sisterly concern.

'No! Everything's not all right,' Esmerelda said. 'That's why I'm here, looking like a Wobbler! Close the gates quickly and I'll tell you.'

They *hurried* inside and the gates slammed shut behind them.

The castle courtyard was lit with flaming torches. Golden statues glinted in the flickery light. Esmerelda couldn't help thinking that the statues were winking at her. Not long till you can have all this lovely gold, they seemed to be saying.

'*Why, thank you,*' Esmerelda said quietly in reply.

'Thank who?' her sister said.

'What? Oh, nothing. I didn't realise I said that out loud. Thank you for letting me in, is what I meant.'

'Don't be silly. You're always welcome here. Now, what's this about the Evil Army? Is my Beatrix safe?' Isabella said, in a worried voice. 'Why isn't she with you? Where is she?'

'Of course she's safe. Don't worry about her – I'd

never let anything bad happen to her.' Esmerelda smiled what she hoped was a reassuring smile. Lying was so easy. All you had to do was say something that wasn't true and wait for people to believe you. 'But the palace has been destroyed, and now the Evil Army is on their way here.'

'So where is she?' Isabella said, her voice growing more high-pitched. 'Where's my daughter?'

Esmerelda thought quickly. If Isabella wanted another lie she could dish one up, no problem. It was like handing out marshmallows – people gobbled them up. 'Beatrix is hiding in a cave in the Dark Dark Woods. But don't tell anyone. It's near one of those new squashed-meatball-in-a-bun cafes, so she won't be hungry. They might get a bit sick of squashed meatballs though. But it's you I'm worried about. My little sister-wister,' Esmerelda said, in her most sincere, non-lying voice. 'Didn't you hear me when I said the Evil Army were on their way here?'

'Yes, yes of course I did. It's just so much to take in. Come, we must get you inside. Tell me what we need to do to prepare for their attack. I shall wake my husband.'

'You do that. And after I've had a nice bath and some hot food I'll tell you what you need to do.'

'Shouldn't we get ready straight away?' Isabella said.

'Oh, they're still quite far from here. At least a day's ride. *Plenty* of time for me to get cleaned up and have some food.'

20

Esmerelda's Evil Plan

A short while later, Esmerelda the Terrible was relaxing in an enormous golden bathtub in front of a fire, in one of the castle's one hundred bedrooms. Isabella's chef had prepared a plate of fartinpants with bacon on the side and plenty of golden syrup, and she ate these slowly, savouring the sweetness.

Eventually she got out of the bath, chose a particularly fine dress from the cupboard, woven with gold and jewels, and went to meet her sister and King Harold. He'd been pacing up and down outside the room, anxious to find out where

Beatrix was and what they needed to do to get ready for the Evil Army's attack.

'Esmerelda, how wonderful to see you,' King Harold said when Esmerelda finally emerged from her room.

'Yes, it is isn't it?' Esmerelda said, stroking her long clean hair and glancing in one of the mirrors along the hallway.

'Isabella tells me Beatrix is hiding in the woods with Ivan,' Harold continued. 'I do hope she's safe. I'm going to send soldiers to protect them – where are they?'

'No need to send anyone – they're quite safe,' said Esmerelda. 'I think the best thing you can do is gather all your soldiers together in the Great

Hall, so I can tell everyone about the Evil Army.'

'All of them?' King Harold said.

'All of them,' Esmerelda said. 'It'll be much quicker that way, believe me.' *Quicker for me to take over your castle*, she thought.

'What about the ones guarding the gates?'

'Especially those ones. They need to know what to look out for. The Evil Army are probably going to try and get past you with some cunning disguises.'

'Very well,' Harold said.

He ordered his servants to round up all his soldiers. Esmerelda watched with satisfaction as they all marched into the enormous Great Hall. The clink and clank of armour and a low mumble of voices filled the air.

Harold looked at the soldiers gathered before him. 'A-hem,' he said, clearing his throat. 'Thank you all for gathering here. I know that some of you were sleeping. Nice pyjamas, by the way.'

He pointed at a soldier in the front row who was wearing a pair of pyjamas with a picture of a Wobbler on the front. The soldier yawned.

'My sister-in-law, the protector of Queen Beatrix, has an important message for us. I want you all to listen very carefully. So please stop chatting at the back.'

The hall fell silent.

King Harold turned, expecting to see Esmerelda, but she wasn't there. *That's strange*, he thought. He heard the sound of the big wooden doors to the Great Hall closing. He turned to Isabella. 'Where's she gone?' he whispered.

'She said she needed to go to the loo,' Isabella replied.

'Really?' said King Harold. He shrugged. 'Well she'd better hurry up,' he said.

Esmerelda ran as fast she could to the city gates and turned the enormous wooden wheel that opened them. Then she grabbed a flaming torch from the wall and ran up the spiral staircase to the top of the tower. She held the torch high and waved it back and forth, then threw it to the ground. In the distance she could see movement. It looked as if the forest was coming towards her. The trees had uprooted themselves and were running towards the castle. Some of them were even riding on cows.

Esmerelda felt an evil laugh, a giant Wooha-ha! growing inside her. She covered her mouth to try and stop it, but she couldn't. It was too big, too loud – it was like an enormous fizzy burp. 'WooHA HAH HAH AHHHA HAAA...' The laugh echoed round the walls of the castle.

It's so good being bad, she thought excitedly. There really wasn't a nicer feeling than the feeling of an Evil Plan going her way.

21

A Human Kebab

In the middle of Wobbler Woods, Oi, Wilfred, Beatrix and the Wobblers were seated round the fire, discussing the best way to get to Beluga. They'd decided it was too risky to try to fly the balloon – the wind could change and send them in the wrong direction. They would bring it with them, though. It could prove useful if they needed to launch an attack from the air.

'I know the woods better than anyone, and I'm

sure there's a short cut to Beluga,' Peter said. 'It's called the Path of Howling Wolves.'

'Well that sounds great,' Oi said. 'The Path of Howling Wolves through the middle of Wobbler Woods. Are you sure there isn't a more dangerous path we should take? Hungry Lion Lane? Deadly Slug Road?'

'Don't be ridiculous,' Peter said. 'There aren't any lions in the woods and slugs eat lettuce, not people. At least as far as I know.'

'Are there a lot of wolves?' Beatrix asked.

'Judging by the howls, I'd say there are...' Peter counted on his fingers. 'A lot,' he said at last. 'But as long as you've got some chewing gum, you'll be fine. Especially strawberry flavour. Wolves love strawberry flavour chewing gum and once they're chewing that, you've got three and a half minutes to make your escape.'

(Chewing gum in the olden days was made from a special kind of tree sap that was all rubbery, which they rolled in strawberry jam.)

There was a rustling sound in the bushes and Peter jumped up, his spear in one hand.

Beatrix turned. On the edge of the clearing were two shadowy figures on horseback. A woman spoke in a nervous voice:

'Hurry up and introduce yourself before that young Wobbler throws a spear and turns you into a human kebab!'

'All right, don't rush me. I'm very stiff – it's been a long day's ride,' a deep voice answered.

Beatrix jumped up. 'Uncle Ivan, is that you?'

Ivan slid off his horse and ran towards his niece.

'Beatrix! There you are!'

'You found us!' she said, as he picked her up and spun her round. Mrs Fartinpants gave her a great big hug too.

'He's been worried sick about you,' she said. 'Off his food for the last week, would you believe it?'

'Ivan off his food?' Wilfred said. 'Never!'

'It was nothing – just a tummy bug. I do feel suddenly better now though,' Ivan said.

'How did you find us?' asked Oi.

'We followed a path through the woods to that balloon thing flapping in the trees, fast as we could. What's happened? Why are you only in Wobbler Woods? Did you get lost?'

Beatrix frowned. 'Not exactly,' she said. 'It's a long story. We had a slight delay at Riddletown. We had to defeat the Riddletown Dragon and free children from General Burpintime's marshmallow factory.'

'You had to what?!' Uncle Ivan said.

'Then we had to find a boat to take us to Beluga, escape from that boat once we discovered it was owned by a pirate, row to Devil Sprout Island then get away from there by  inventing the world's first hot-air balloon, which we crashed in Wobbler Woods last night. So here we are. Not much nearer to Beluga at all.'

'Sounds like you've been busy,' Mrs Fartinpants said. 'I'll get some fartinpants on the go. I bet you're hungry.'

'Thank you, that would be lovely. You

do make the best fartinpants. Now you and Uncle Ivan are here we can go to Beluga with all your soldiers and protect my mother and father's castle from the Evil Army,' Beatrix said. At last she was starting to feel as if things might be all right. 'Where are they, by the way?' Beatrix squinted into the bushes, trying to see them.

'Where are who??' Ivan replied.

'Your soldiers,' Beatrix said. 'I must say they're being very quiet – it's most impressive.'

Uncle Ivan frowned. 'They're not here. Your note didn't say anything about bringing my army. Anyway, your mother and father have ten thousand extremely well-trained soldiers and very high castle walls. General Burpintime won't be able to break into the castle.'

'No, he won't. But he's got Esmerelda with him, and she won't need to break in. She can just knock on the front door.'

Uncle Ivan's hand hovered over the knife in

his belt. Before you could say *Wait a minute, there are children here, it's not a good idea to start throwing knives about*, he'd thrown it into a nearby tree.

'Can everyone stop throwing sharp objects at that poor tree?' Oi said.

'If they've already taken over the castle, we won't need an army, we'll need a miracle,' Ivan said.

'How about fifteen wobblers, a balloon, Wilfred's magic and some strawberry chewing gum?' Beatrix said.

Uncle Ivan looked puzzled. 'Why do we need strawberry chewing gum?'

Somewhere in the distance a wolf howled the howliest howl any of them had ever heard.

'To keep the jaws of the wolves busy,' Beatrix replied.

22

A Long Walk, a Run, some more Walking, and a bit more Running

Early next morning, Beatrix, Ivan, Mrs Fartinpants, Oi the Boy, Dog the dog, Wilfred the Wise and fifteen Wobblers set off with their Balloon of Doom and their strawberry chewing gum along the Path of Howling Wolves. The Wobblers had rolled up the balloon and were carrying it on their shoulders. It had taken them a while to work out how to get it down from the tree, then Ivan picked up an axe and showed them that it might be easier if they got the tree down first.

They ran as *fast* as they could for as long as they could. Then they walked and they walked and threw some more chewing gum at the wolves, then they ran, and then they walked some more.

The night passed and the sun rose but they barely noticed. On and on they went. Even though

it was a short cut, it was still a *very* long journey. They didn't stop till lunch time the next day, and then they only paused for a few minutes to scoff some fartinpants. They walked for another day and another night and another day. By the end of the fourth day, Beatrix was starting to worry that this wasn't a short cut at all.

'Are we nearly there yet?' Beatrix said.

'We're not far now,' Peter replied. 'This is the edge of the forest. Once we pass those trees up ahead you'll see the walls that surround the city of Beluga. The castle's in the middle.'

'We should stop here then,' Beatrix said. She looked around for a tree to climb. 'Let's get a good look at Beluga before it gets dark,' she said.

Oi, Beatrix and Peter climbed up a tall tree at the edge of the forest. In the distance they could see the walled city with the castle at the centre. High stone walls encircled it. There were lots of houses in between the walls and the castle, with little streets running between them. It looked as if the houses had all gathered round the castle for protection, like little animals staying close to their mother. To the south of the castle was the port, where sailing ships were moored. Beatrix could see stables and a large market square, but there weren't many people around.

'Can anyone see anything that looks a bit unusual?' Beatrix said, looking for a sign that the castle had been taken over by the Evil Army.

'Like what?' Peter said.

'I don't know. Evil Army soldiers in disguise? Something like that. It all seems very quiet.'

'Nope,' said Peter. 'Seems pretty normal to me. I can see Beluga Army soldiers – they don't look very happy though, they look pretty angry. Two of them over there are *arguing* about something, look.' He pointed at two soldiers standing in the large square in front of the castle. One of them was eating a sandwich and the other kept pointing at it and shaking his head.

'What's that one doing over there?' Oi said. 'It looks like he's washing the paint off a herd of cows. Or horses. Or are they zebras? Whatever they are, he's washing the paint off.'

'Zebras?!' said Beatrix. She looked to where Oi was pointing. The horses that the Evil Army had painted black and white to disguise them as cows had been caught in the rain, and were now streaked with black and white paint. A soldier with a brush was trying to clean them.

Beatrix drew a deep breath. 'The Evil Army is here. Those aren't my parents' soldiers. I know it. Only an Evil Army soldier would argue over a sandwich like that.' She turned away and climbed back down the tree.

'They're here,' she said to Ivan and Wilfred when she reached the bottom. 'The Evil Army is in Beluga. I don't know what they've done to my father and mother but I'm going to find out.' Somehow she felt as if this was her fault, that she'd put her parents in danger.

'We'll defeat them. I'll go back to the palace and get my army and we'll lay siege to the castle,' Ivan said. 'They don't call me Ivan the Vicious for nothing, you know.'

'There's no time,' said Beatrix. 'The longer

we leave it, the more chance there is of something terrible happening to my parents.'

Oi jumped down from the last few branches.

'So what's the plan?' he said.

Beatrix frowned. 'I was thinking I'd just hand myself over to the Evil Army. It's the quickest way to end this.'

'Oh, right,' Oi replied, looking a little puzzled. 'And then what?'

Beatrix smiled. She looked at the rolled-up balloon the Wobblers had carried through the woods.

'And then we make the Curse of the Wobblers come true, with a little help from the Balloon of Doom, Peter and his gang and, of course, Mrs Fartinpants. How long do you think it will take you to make five hundred fartinpants, Mrs Fartinpants?'

Mrs Fartinpants shrugged. 'My record is three fartinpants a minute, so that would be...'

'About a hundred and sixty-six minutes,' Beatrix said, as Mrs Fartinpants counted on her fingers.

'Why do we need so many fartinpants?' Ivan said. 'I can only eat two a minute – it'd take me ages to get through that many.'

'Because after I've handed myself over to the Evil Army, you and Oi are going to turn up with a big delivery of fartinpants and ask to be let in.'

'Oh, right,' Oi said. 'Who ordered the fartinpants?'

'No one! It's a *trick*. You'll tell

them someone ordered a takeaway. They'll let you in. No one can turn down a fartinpant. Certainly not a whole sackful. Once you're inside you'll have to do four things. This is important – are you listening?'

'I'm listening,' Ivan said.

'I'm listening,' Oi said. 'And definitely *not* thinking about eating all those fartinpants.'

23

One Hundred and Two Ways to Eat a Marshmallow

The winter sun rose early, casting its pale yellow light through the tall windows and across the enormous library where General Burpintime was sitting reading. He'd taken a bath in Queen Isabella's golden bathtub, which was almost the size of a swimming pool. He'd eaten a delicious breakfast of marshmallows on toast prepared by the *excellent* chefs in the kitchen, and now he was relaxing by the fire, and still wearing his pyjamas (it felt very much like a pyjama day).

The book he was reading was called *One Hundred and Two Ways to Eat a Marshmallow*, and it was the sequel to his favourite book *One Hundred and One Ways to Eat a Marshmallow*. As he sat and perused the pages, he was feeling rather pleased with himself. Queen Isabella, her husband and the entire army were locked up in the Great Hall, and he had control of Beluga. His boss, the Evil Overlord, would be happy. In fact, he'd already sent a messenger to tell him how well everything was going. He flexed his toes by the fire, enjoying the warmth and the comfy snuggle of the soft pyjamas he'd borrowed (or should I say *stolen*) from King Harold.

Even Esmerelda was being less annoying than normal. Instead of bossing him about, she seemed to be bossing about his army instead, telling them where to stand guard, making sure they were disguised as soldiers from the Beluga Army in case Beatrix arrived. It was as if she thought they were *her* army! That was fine with General Burpintime – he needed a little peace and quiet after all the adventures of the last few weeks.

All he had to do now was wait for the arrival of Beatrix. As soon as she turned up asking to see her parents he'd take her prisoner. Easy-peasy. He flicked through the pages in his book. He was reading about how to make a very tasty-sounding marshmallow omelette when one of his guards knocked on the door.

'There's a young girl at the castle gates,' he announced, stepping into the room. 'She says she's Beatrix the Bold and that she's here to see her parents.'

General Burpintime jumped upright with a sudden jolt. 'Whaty-wot-wot-whaty-who?' he said.

'She said she's Beatrix the Bold and she wants to see her parents.'

'And she's here on her own – right here, no Wobblers, no army? There's no pigeon with her, is there, or dog?' General Burpintime shivered as he remembered how Jeff and Dog had attacked him and ruined his dragon costume.

'No dog, no pigeon. No Wobblers. Just a girl in some rather ragged clothes who looks like a bird's made a nest in her hair.'

General Burpintime rubbed his hands together. He could barely contain his excitement.

'Bring her into the castle, quick as you can. Don't let her get away. Then take her to the dungeons. You'll need chains. And a cage. She's a slippery one. Chain her to the cage. No wait – tie her up first, then chain her inside the cage. Then lock the dungeon door. And guard the door. We don't want her to escape. Are you sure there are no Wobblers?'

General Burpintime didn't wait for an answer. Still in his pyjamas, he ran as fast as he could to the balcony at the front of the castle. He stared at the small girl standing by the gates. The last time he'd seen her it was dark and she'd been standing by a marshmallow boat in the River Riddle. He hadn't been able to get a good look at her. Now he stood and he stared, shielding his eyes against

the sun. Beatrix the Bold. Walking right into his trap. Expecting to see her parents and instead all she was going to see was the inside of a dungeon.

'Ha-Ha-Ha, HA-HA-HA, A-HAA-HAA HAA!'

'What on earth is that noise?' A voice came from behind him. Esmerelda. 'You sound like you're about to sneeze your head off. That'd be just like you, catching a cold because you've had a little walk through the mountains.' She came to stand next to Burpintime.

'Ah, I see,' she said, looking out over the courtyard. Her niece was standing there. 'She's here. My plan worked. I'll take that carriage full of gold to go, please. Get it ready at once.'

24

The Star of the Show

Beatrix stared up at the huge castle. It loomed over the houses around it like a friendly giant, protective but slightly forbidding too. *My castle*, she thought. She hoped her parents were safe.

She stood and waited, and if she could have crossed her fingers she would have done so. (You can't cross your fingers when you're carrying out a dangerous plan to retake your parents' castle, it sort of gives the game away – so she crossed her toes instead.)

'Come 'ere, young lady,' said the guard from the Evil Army. He was very uncomfortable because he was wearing two uniforms. His normal Evil Army uniform and his Beluga uniform over the top. He was also carrying a thick rope and some chains, which were very heavy.

'You need to come with me into the castle. I'm going to take you to meet your parents, and you don't need to be afraid. No one's going to tie you up and put you in a cage or prison or anything.' The guard frowned. He wasn't sure if he was supposed to say that.

'Of course they're not. Why would they? Just out of interest, what are those chains and ropes for?' Beatrix asked with an innocent smile.

'Er, fixing things,' the guard said. 'Things that have, you know, fallen off.'

'How wonderful. I love fixing things too, and I'm so pleased to be here,' Beatrix said in the biggest, smiliest voice she could manage. She wanted to show that she wasn't at all suspicious of the soldier, even though he was an extremely suspicious character. She decided to have some fun with him instead. 'Seeing as I'm going to be Queen of Beluga, don't you think you should bow down on one knee to me?'

'Um.' The guard looked over his shoulder at the castle, as if someone there might tell him what to do.

'All right,' he said, bending down. The ropes and chains looked as if they were very heavy.

'Bit lower,' Beatrix said.

The guard bent down even further.

'Tiny bit lower,' Beatrix said.

The guard nearly fell forwards and put a hand out to stop himself.

'Perfect!' Beatrix said, clapping her hands together. 'Shall we go and see my parents?'

The guard got up and brushed the dust off his knees. 'This way,' he said, grumpily.

He led Beatrix along the main street towards the huge wooden doors at the entrance to the castle. He was thinking how easy it was to capture this queen, and how silly the Evil Army had been for believing in the Curse of the Wobblers. He didn't even need to tie her up and carry her in – she didn't suspect a thing.

He opened a heavy wooden door and told Beatrix to walk down the narrow passageway.

'This way,' he said again.

'What a nice cosy passageway,' Beatrix said.

'In there,' the guard muttered after they had gone a short distance. He pointed into a small cell with no windows and a large cage in the middle.

'Oh, how lovely,' Beatrix said. A rat looked up from the corner of the room where it was chewing on a piece of straw, twitched its nose, then carried on chewing. 'A pet rat! How did you know they were my *favourite* animal? And a Wendy house for me to play in!'

She ran towards the cage and climbed inside. 'It's so lovely. I can tell I'm going to have the best time in the world in here! Do hurry along and find my mother and father, so they can play with me too.'

The guard frowned. A *Wendy house*? A *pet rat*?! He decided the girl was the strangest young lady he'd ever met. Then again, he hadn't met any

queens before. Maybe they were all like this. A bit
dotty. He reached forward, swung the cage door
shut and hooked an enormous padlock through it.

'And it even has a lock, so I'm safe and secure!'
Beatrix said as he clicked the padlock shut. The
guard left the room and locked the door behind
him.

'I'll be back in a few minutes,' he shouted.
'Someone wants to see you.'

'Lovely! I hope it's my mummy and daddy!' Beatrix called out after him. She knew it wouldn't be, but as she said the words she suddenly felt a mixture of fear and excitement. She was so close now, so close to finally seeing them again!

It wasn't long before she heard footsteps echo along the corridor outside and someone whistling cheerfully. A key turned in the lock, and the door creaked as it swung open slowly.

General Burpintime entered the room, and he was so happy he almost danced towards the cage. Beatrix the Bold was right here, in his castle. And it was perfectly clear she had no magical powers whatsoever. And no Wobblers. Today was a good day to be General Burpintime. The Evil Overlord would be so pleased!

He bent down next to the cage and peered inside.

'Hello, Chef. Have you brought me some nice food?' Beatrix said.

'I am not a chef!' General Burpintime replied. 'I'm General Burpintime, leader of the Evil Army from Beyond the Woods, marshmallow-eating champion, supreme swimmer with four swimming badges – including doggy paddle – inventor of the horse ski, master of the recorder and undefeated in every battle I've ever fought.'

Beatrix was quiet for a moment. Then she said: 'Are you sure you're undefeated in every battle?'

'Yes. Of course.'

'*Every* battle?'

'Yes.'

'Even the one where the Wobblers chased you out of your tent in the middle of the night?'

'How on earth do you know about that? And anyway, it wasn't even a battle. It was more of a strange nightmare.'

'I suppose you've never been defeated by a dog or a pigeon, either?'

General Burpintime drew a deep breath. Who

did she think she was, questioning him? She was the one trapped in a cage. In a dungeon. In a castle he'd just captured. There was NO WAY she could win this.

'You're my prisoner, and, tomorrow morning, I'm going to put that cage with you in it in the middle of the courtyard on a specially-constructed stage, and show all the Evil Army that I've captured you and prevented the Curse of the Wobblers from coming true. And after that we're going to have a massive party.'

'I *love* parties!' Beatrix said.

'Not you. You're going to work night and day rebuilding my marshmallow factory. Then you're going to work day and night making my marshmallows.'

'And then I'm going to eat all your marshmallows.'

'And then you're going to eat my marshmallows.' General Burpintime paused, his face became angry. 'And then you're NOT going to eat any marshmallows. Ever again. Because you'll be dead. Ha!'

'I don't like them that much anyway.' Beatrix yawned and stretched her arms in the little cage. 'Would you mind fetching a blanket and throwing it over the cage?' she said. 'I'd like to have a rest before my big show tomorrow. I can't wait. Everyone will be looking at me. It'll be great to be the star.'

'You're not the star! I'm the star. It's my show. Except it's not a show. It's an important public ceremony to mark the end of the Curse of the Wobblers. Followed by a big party.'

He stood straight and puffed out his chest. *It is my show*, he told himself. *My big moment*. He wasn't about to let a silly little girl steal it from him.

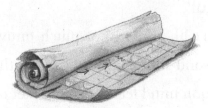

25

Two Sore Heads

Outside the city walls, Uncle Ivan and Oi were trying their hardest not to eat any of the delicious-smelling fartinpants they were carrying. They were still warm, and the warmth made them even more tempting.

Ivan banged impatiently on the tall wooden gates.

'What do you want?' shouted an angry voice from the top of the gate tower.

'Good morning,' Uncle Ivan said. 'We're here to deliver these bags of fartinpants. Someone in the castle ordered a takeaway from the bakery in the woods. Someone very greedy. Anyone like that in the castle?'

The guard stared down at Oi and Ivan. The fartinpants smelt delicious. There were lots of greedy people in the castle. And they all liked to use pigeons to order takeaway food from the woods.

'Who ordered the fartinpants?' he said.

'Didn't quite get the name,' Ivan replied. 'Sounded like Burps-a-lot or Trumps-in-time or something. Hurry up and open up. We don't want them to get cold, do we?' He threw one up and the guard caught it and ate it greedily.

The gates swung open and Ivan and Oi stepped inside.

'Well, that was easy,' Ivan said.

'Easy if you've got a super-fast cook to make fartinpants and a Beatrix the Bold to come up with a plan to get you into the castle,' Oi said.

'Oh, yes. I suppose so. Now the part I'm really looking forward to – finding a couple of Evil Army soldiers whose uniforms we can steal.'

Ivan looked around. There were lots of soldiers. They were disguised as soldiers from the Beluga Army, but you could just see the markings of the red and black Evil Army uniform underneath.

'Those two over there look roughly the right size. Let's see if I can persuade them to hand over their uniforms.' Ivan cracked his knuckles, clenched his fists and grinned.

A few moments later, the two guards were stripped to their Evil Army underpants and stuffed in barrels. Ivan looked very pleased with himself. Oi looked a little taken aback. He knew that Ivan's name was Ivan the Vicious, but he'd never actually seen him performing full-on Kung-fu ninja moves on enemy soldiers.

'They'll be fine,' Uncle Ivan said, as he put the
lids on the barrels and made a little air hole in the
top with his knife. 'Just a little bit stiff when they
wake up. And with a sore head. But if you join the
Evil Army you've got to expect to get knocked
out, tied up and stuffed in a barrel. It's what you
get paid for.'

'I don't think they'll be waking up for a while,'

 Oi said. 'Let's put on both sets of uniforms and complete number two on our to-do list – find Beatrix's mother and father.'

They put on the uniforms, then walked across the large courtyard in front of the castle. Whenever they met a soldier from the Evil Army, they muttered a mean-sounding insult, which was exactly how Evil Army soldiers were supposed to greet one another. Uncle Ivan gave them a friendly punch on the arm too. This wasn't how Evil Army soldiers were meant to greet one another, but Ivan couldn't resist hitting them whenever he saw them.

It didn't take them long to find out where Beatrix's parents were hidden. Oi simply put on his best Evil Army voice and asked another Evil Army soldier where they were.

'Hey, stupid,' he said. 'I can't remember where we put the King and Queen of Beluga.'

'They're locked in the Great Hall, you idiot,' the soldier said, thinking Oi really must be an idiot.

'And all their soldiers, are they in the same place?'

'Of course! Where *else* would they be?'

'I dunno – I thought maybe they'd be in the dungeon.'

'We can't put them in the dungeons. There are too many of them. And anyway, those cells are reserved for Beatrix the Bold. Can't you remember anything?'

'Afraid not. I must be a real dumb-dumb head,' said Oi. 'Just out of interest, if I wanted to find the Great Hall, I would go...'

'Through the main doors of the castle, up the big wooden staircase with the gold statues, along the corridor of many mirrors, past the big painting of a small dog, then it's right in front of you. Two massive wooden doors with a bolt across. You can't miss it.'

'That's great. Thank you,' Oi said. 'Did you get all that?' he asked Ivan.

Ivan had taken out a piece of paper and was making notes in charcoal. 'Yes, got all that.'

'Oh, and one more thing,' Oi said, turning back to the soldier. 'If we wanted to find the dungeon…'

'You go through the door on the left in the main hall of the castle, down the stairs, along the narrow passage and you'll see a row of cells right in front of you. *Honestly*, the guard muttered to himself as he walked away. '*They'll let anyone into the Evil Army these days.*'

They followed the instructions Ivan had written down and found the Great Hall. There were four soldiers from the Evil Army standing guard outside.

'Bad mornin',' said Oi in his best Evil Army voice.

'Bad mornin' to you too,' the soldier replied.

'Everything all right here?' Oi asked. 'They're not giving you any trouble in there, are they?' He could hear lots of grumbling and angry voices coming from inside, all muffled and soupy.

'They banged a lot on the doors at first, but most of them are in their pyjamas and they don't have any weapons. And they're quite tired now as we haven't given them any food for two days. Ha ha ha.'

'Yes, ha ha ha,' Ivan said, punching the soldier on the arm in a friendly but also slightly painful

way. 'Good for you. You guards have done a great job. You can have the rest of the day off. We'll take over now.'

If anyone else had said this, it wouldn't have sounded very convincing, but because Uncle Ivan was a very large man with a very deep voice who was used to telling soldiers what to do, the soldiers did what he said. They even thanked him.

'Not at all. It's me who should be thanking you,' Ivan said, with a twinkle in his eye. 'Here are some fartinpants for all your hard work.' He handed them a couple each and they walked away feeling very pleased with themselves. Once they'd gone he turned to Oi.

'I'm going in, you wait outside.'

26

Esmerelda the Terrible
Decides Not to Change her Name

Esmerelda hurried along the narrow corridor towards Beatrix's cell. She wanted to see if her niece really was in the cage. It had been so easy to capture her this time. She peered through the small window in the cell door. A figure was squashed inside a cage. Esmerelda felt a strange pain in her chest, the same as she had when she arrived at her sister's castle, the same as she had after eating too many fartinpants. Then she remembered the carriage full of gold that was waiting for her in the courtyard of the palace and the pain started to go away. She walked quickly from the dungeon.

Well, they do call me Esmerelda the Terrible, she thought, *so it's not as if I should let her escape. If I did, I wouldn't be terrible any more, and I'd have to change my name.*

Esmerelda the Not-So-Terrible-Any-More just didn't sound as good.

After Esmerelda had gone, a guard turned up with a blanket which he threw over the top of Beatrix's cage. Beatrix said thank you in the same sunny voice she'd been using since she arrived, and tried not to think about everything that could go wrong with her plan.

Technically, she was locked in a cage, that was locked in a dungeon, inside a castle that had been taken over by the Evil Army. And she had let General Burpintime do this. Her stomach felt fluttery and her head felt dizzy at this thought. But it was all part of her plan. However mad it seemed, and however dangerous, she was the one in control. (Even though she was *technically* locked in a cage in a dungeon).

27

Night Falls

As night fell, the Wobblers, Wilfred and Mrs Fartinpants became very busy indeed. In a clearing in the woods they carefully unrolled the Balloon of Doom and checked to see if the basket was damaged. The sky had cleared and the moon shone brightly as they mixed up black paint using charcoal from the fire; and made red paint using clay from a nearby river bank. They soaked the huge balloon in black paint, then added an enormous angry face in red.

It was the kind of face you might see on a pumpkin at Halloween. Jagged teeth, fierce eyes with slanty eyebrows and a circle in the middle to show where the Wobbler's third eye had fallen out. Because the black paint wasn't quite dry, the red paint soaked into it, making the big balloon look even more sinister and ghostly. (Although if you stood close to it you could still see a few pairs of pants in it, which they hoped the Evil Army wouldn't notice.)

Then the Wobblers dug a hole in the ground that was slightly smaller than the base of the balloon, just as Beatrix had told them, and prepared a fire so it would be ready for launching in the morning.

Meanwhile, inside the castle, Ivan the Vicious was on his way to Beatrix's cell. This was item number four on his to-do list and it was very satisfying to have ticked off the first three already.

He crept up on the guard outside, and was about to bash him on the head when he remembered that there was a much easier way to make an Evil Army soldier do what you want.

'Good evening, you fat-bottomed old fool,' he said.

The guard turned.

'Good evening to you too, pooh head,' the guard replied.

'I'm taking over now,' Ivan said, peering in through the narrow window in the door. *Poor Beatrix, stuck in that tiny cage*, he thought. He could feel his fists clench, and was almost tempted to bash the soldier on the head anyway. 'Give me the keys for the cell and the cage.'

The guard looked at Ivan, shrugged, and handed over the keys. Ivan gave him another of his friendly punches on the arm, even harder than last time.

'Have a fartinpant too, for all your hard work,' he said.

The guard took one and hurried off, rubbing his arm.

Ivan checked to see no one was coming, then went quickly into the cell.

'How are you? Not too squashed?' he whispered as he opened the cage.

Beatrix climbed out, stretching her stiff limbs, and gave him a hug. 'Pretty squashed. Thank goodness you're here!' she said. 'I was starting to worry something had gone *wrong*. Did you find my father and mother?'

'Yes, they're in the Great Hall. We've got rid of the guards, it's just Oi outside now.'

'Have you got the Wobbler outfit and the fartinpants?' Beatrix asked.

'Right here,' Ivan said, opening up the sack.

Beatrix quickly slipped out of her clothes and put on the animal skins so she looked like one of

the Wobblers, then she and Uncle Ivan stuffed her
old clothes full of fartinpants and put them back
into the cage.

They locked the cage and Beatrix threw the blanket back over it. Then they left the dungeon and locked the door. Beatrix climbed into the sack Uncle Ivan had brought the fartinpants in. He hung the keys up outside the cell, picked up the sack with Beatrix in and lifted it carefully over his shoulder. He walked back along the corridor, then carried Beatrix across the courtyard, muttering friendly insults to the Evil Army soldiers who were standing guard. Even though it was way past midnight, people were still up, hammering together the stage for General Burpintime to stand on for his big ceremony.

Ivan carried Beatrix all the way up to the top of the gatehouse tower. He put her down carefully and opened the top of the sack.

'All set?' he said.

'All set,' Beatrix replied. 'Now we just wait till morning.'

28

The Big Show
that Wasn't a Show

As day was breaking, soldiers from the Evil Army opened the door to Beatrix's cell, lifted up the cage (which felt a bit lighter, but not too light) and carried it to the large courtyard in front of the castle. They felt very hungry as they did, because they kept smelling delicious fartinpants, but they assumed someone was baking them in the kitchen. They put the cage on the large wooden stage General Burpintime had built in the middle of the castle courtyard.

The courtyard in front of the castle soon filled up with ten thousand very excited soldiers from the Evil Army. They were all trying their hardest not to look like they were having a good time, because they always had to look angry, but the truth was they loved to gather together, watch a show and have a chat. General Burpintime had put banners up all round the courtyard with big pictures of a Wobbler with a cross through it on them. Today was the day he was going to tell everyone that the Curse of the Wobblers had been broken.

At the side of the stage, a band was playing traditional Evil Army songs. The band was called *The Killers*, and they'd named themselves after the Evil Army's favourite word (KILL!). Most of their songs had the word 'kill' in them too, like 'Killing Me Killing You, A-ha', 'Kill Me Do' and the classic 'A View to a Kill'.

There were stalls giving away cakes and squashed-meatball-in-buns and it felt more like a festival than an important Victory Speech. General Burpintime stood on the balcony looking out over the courtyard, and breathed deeply. He was a very happy man. Even the sudden arrival of Esmerelda next to him didn't annoy him.

'Are you ready for your little show?' she said.

'It's not a little show. It's actually quite a big show. Are you going to stay and watch?'

'No. I'm going to take my carriage full of gold, find a nice spot to build a castle and…' She paused. She had a few ideas of  her own but she wasn't about to share these with General Burpintime.

'Good. I'd like to say it's been a pleasure working with you,' General Burpintime said with a smile. 'But I can't because it hasn't. Goodbye.'

General Burpintime couldn't wait for her to go. He didn't even mind giving her the gold. It was a small price to pay to get rid of her and, anyway, he didn't have to pay it himself. He'd used Queen Isabella's gold.

He put on his finest uniform and pinned all his medals across his chest (including those he'd won for stuffing the most marshmallows in his mouth). He combed his moustache, flattened down his eyebrows and strode down the steps to the courtyard.

A huge cheer arose from the crowd. He raised a hand and saluted them, walking slowly to the stage, enjoying the moment. He felt proud, and at least a foot taller. (Which meant he was now almost six foot tall!) He stood in the centre of the stage, tapping his foot to the music, whipped out his recorder and played a quick solo, then signalled for the band to stop.

His ten thousand soldiers stood before him

and Beatrix the Bold was in a cage covered in a blanket, right next to him. All was well in the world, and life felt good – in fact, life felt so good it was as if the very air smelt of delicious fartinpants. He really should have brought his artist with him. This was another of those moments that would feature in the book of his life. A double pager.

Burpintime turned to his soldiers, and pulled out the piece of paper on which he'd written his speech.

'Soldiers of the Evil Army,' he said in his high voice. 'Today is an important day. Today is the day we put an end to the Curse of the Wobblers. For years we've lived in fear of a queen who will take over our land with an army of Wobblers. Well, those days are no more. Using my exception-ally brilliant soldier skills, I have captured Beatrix the Bold. The curse is gone. I have won. Beatrix is in this cage, under this blanket!'

There was silence from the crowd; ten thousand pairs of eyes looked at him expectantly.

'This is the point where you cheer,' General Burpintime said.

A huge cheer arose from the crowd. He took a step back, grabbed the corner of the cloth that covered the cage and gave it a quick yank.

'Ta-dah!' he said.

The soldiers' cheering grew even louder. General Burpintime waved for them to be quiet.

'Not so clever now, are you, Beatrix the Bold?' He said her name as if it was a piece of broccoli he wanted to spit out.

There was no response from the cage, so General Burpintime knelt down and peered inside. Although he could see Beatrix's clothes, it didn't look much like there was a person inside them. It looked more like a sack of potatoes or cakes.

He unlocked the door and reached in, grabbing hold of Beatrix by the leg. But instead of a leg, he found he was holding a trouserful of fartinpants.

What magic is this? he asked himself. *Some kind*

of trick, some sort of witchcraft? He felt his blood turn cold. Could she turn herself into cakes whenever she wanted to?! He looked out at the crowd of soldiers. They stared directly back at him. Ten thousand pairs of eyes. Panic started to creep over him.

A voice shouted from the top of the tower by the castle gates. A loud voice. A confident voice.

'Soldiers of the Evil Army. I've got some good news, and some bad news,' Beatrix said.

The crowd turned and stared up at her in stunned silence. This *definitely* wasn't part of the show. General Burpintime looked as if he'd just seen a ghost. Or a Wobbler. Or a ghost Wobbler.

'The bad news is that I'm Beatrix the Bold and the Curse of the Wobblers is about to come true. You're going to be defeated by an army of Wobblers and I'm going to take over all of your lands.'

The crowd frowned as if it were one gigantic pair of eyebrows.

'What's the good news?' a voice shouted from the back.

'The good news is that I'm Beatrix the Bold and the Curse of the Wobblers is about to come true.' Beatrix paused. 'Sorry, I should have said that it's good news for me. Not you. Bad news for you. Good news and bad news. Depends whose side you're on. Now, I'll give you one chance to throw down your weapons and join my side.'

The soldiers shuffled about uneasily. They really liked their weapons. And without them what were they? Were they even soldiers? Wouldn't they just be very angry men? They looked at the girl then they looked at General Burpintime. General Burpintime looked into the cage again, just to make doubly sure she wasn't there, then looked at the girl standing on the tower. He still couldn't work out how she'd done it.

'Of course we won't surrender!' he shouted back. 'Where are all these Wobblers? I don't see any!'

'Very well,' Beatrix said. 'If that's the way you want it.'

Beatrix turned her back on the crowd and raised her arms in the air, as if she was about to conduct an orchestra.

29

The Ballunatic of Doom

Outside the castle, the Wobblers, Wilfred the Wise and Mrs Fartinpants were holding onto the ropes of the Balloon of Doom, keeping it as close to the ground as they could. It was filled with hot air and straining like an angry dog on a lead. When they saw Beatrix's signal they climbed inside, pressing themselves into the small basket and hanging over the sides, holding onto the ropes. The balloon rose slowly, peeking over the city walls.

First a round circle that looked a bit like a third eye appeared. Then came two angry red eyes, staring down at the soldiers. The balloon continued to rise. The angry mouth appeared. The soldiers of the Evil Army stepped back, except for those at the back of the crowd, who couldn't step back. They just got a bit squashed instead.

The soldiers had never seen a *real* Wobbler, and they'd certainly never seen one without a body. Or with ropes attached to it. Or with what looked like a pair of pants above one of its eyebrows. The Balloon of Doom rose higher and the basket full of Wobblers came into view.

At the same time, Ivan and Oi unlocked the doors to the Great Hall.

'Follow me,' Ivan shouted. 'It's time to teach these Evil Army soldiers a lesson!'

The Beluga Army charged after him, racing towards the courtyard.

The Wobblers flung ropes over the side of the

basket and were sliding down into the crowd of Evil Army soldiers. Wilfred stayed in the basket, setting fire to fartinpants and flinging them at the soldiers. The Evil Army soldiers charged into one another in confusion, trying to dodge the burning cakes. They tried to find a way out of the courtyard, but the gates were locked.

The battle that followed was short. In fact, it would go down in history as the shortest battle that has ever been fought. It was over in 17.5 seconds. That was even less time than it took Dog and Jeff to trip up the Riddletown Dragon and rip off its head. And less time than it took to scare General Burpintime into *running* out of his tent in the middle of the night. In fact, it was the same amount of time as it takes General Burpintime to eat 17.5 marshmallows. Which was all he'd done since the battle had begun.

How is this happening? he asked himself.

Only a few moments ago Beatrix was locked in the cage. Now it seemed as if the Curse of the Wobblers might be coming true! *No no no no no.* He couldn't think what to do, so he ate another marshmallow.

Beatrix ran down the steps of the tower, pushed her way through the confusion of soldiers and jumped up onto the stage. She stood next to General Burpintime, who turned and stared at her in disbelief.

'I think it's time you told them to surrender,' Beatrix said. 'They're surrounded and they've all thrown down their weapons anyway.'

General Burpintime looked at the soldiers, then looked at Beatrix, then looked up at the Balloon of Doom, which was floating over their heads. There was *no way out* of this one. He sighed a very loud sigh and took out his recorder and played the three-note surrender song, but his soldiers didn't hear him. (They never did – it was the worst way to tell an army to stop fighting.) Instead he shouted at them.

'STOP FIGHTING!'

The soldiers heard him this time and stopped fighting, apart from one or two who never stopped when they were told to stop, like those annoying kids in your class who carry on when the teacher says 'BE QUIET!'

General Burpintime turned to Beatrix and sighed another deep sigh. Then he put his hand into his pocket, took out his last marshmallow and offered it to her. Beatrix took it but she didn't eat it. Not this one. This one was the Marshmallow of Surrender. A white flag. This was a marshmallow to be kept in a glass case in a museum.

Uncle Ivan jumped up on stage. Behind him was a man with a twinkle in his eye and a tall and very beautiful woman with a mass of curly hair. Beatrix knew at once who they were – she recognised them from the portrait in her room at the palace. Her heart felt as if it might burst. She ran towards them as fast as she could.

'You did it!' her mother said, giving her the biggest hug ever. 'You rescued us! You defeated the Evil Army, once and for all. I'm *so* sorry – you've gone through so much, dragons and pirates and the whole Curse of the Wobblers…' Her eyes filled with tears, she was smiling and laughing and crying all at the same time.

Her father placed his hands on her shoulders. 'I wish we hadn't sent you away, but it was too dangerous. You wouldn't have been safe. Not with all the nonsense about you having magic powers.'

'She *does* have magic powers,' a voice piped up from somewhere in the crowd. It was Oi. He pushed his way to the front. 'I've been with her long enough to see it for myself. She can make pants and trousers fly, she can make marshmallow into boats and she can turn a dog into a terrifying Wobbler.'

Her father turned to the crowd.

'Tonight we shall have a feast,' he said. 'Tonight we celebrate the return of our daughter, Beatrix the Bold. Three cheers for Beatrix the Bold! *Hip hip –*'

'LET ME DOWN!' a voice shouted before anyone could say 'Hooray!'

The crowd looked up. The Balloon of Doom was caught on the high tower of the castle. Wilfred was inside, his hands gripped tightly onto the edge of the basket.

'Hurry up! It's going to tear!' he shouted. The balloon had deflated and looked like a big black and red cloth, draped over the tower.

'We'll have you down in a jiffy!' Beatrix's father shouted.

A group of Beluga Army soldiers climbed quickly up the walls with ropes to rescue Wilfred, and the rest of the soldiers collected up all the weapons from the Evil Army. They tied up General Burpintime so he couldn't escape.

'What do we do now?' said one of the Evil Army soldiers.

30

The Fantastic Feast

That night, a fantastic feast was laid out on the tables in the Great Hall. There were squashed-meatballs-in-buns, fresh fartinpants, bowls of marshmallows and Beluga Pies, which weren't pies, but were like a big, open sandwich with melted cheese and tomato on top. (Basically a 'pizza', before pizzas had been invented.)

Hundreds of candles were placed on the tables and bunting and banners hung from the walls.

The Evil Army band had renamed themselves *The Beatrix the Bold Band*, and were now playing songs that were much more tuneful and didn't have the word 'KILL' in the chorus.

All in all, it was a joyous event, and all the more so for Beatrix and her father and mother, who were sitting at the top table. Beatrix sat on the throne in the middle, with her mother and father on either side and Ivan, Wilfred, Oi, Mrs Fartinpants, Dog the dog and the Wobblers around her.

She had sent soldiers to try and find Esmerelda and had told the guards to put General Burpintime in one of the dungeons. Then she decided it would be more fun if he had to work in the kitchens, making marshmallows he wasn't allowed to eat, so she moved him there.

Although he was extremely grumpy about this, he was very good at making marshmallows and in many ways a natural chef. He liked to boss people about, was good at planning and had an excellent memory for recipes. He could remember every single one of the 102 ways to eat a marshmallow and had made a very tasty marshmallow ice-cream, as well as marshmallow muffins, which Beatrix was now enjoying.

'This is delicious!' Beatrix said as she tucked into her second bowl of muffins and ice-cream. 'I think we should make General Burpintime work in the kitchens for the rest of his life. He's clearly *very* talented.'

'Certainly is,' Oi said. He looked thoughtfully at his reflection in the back of his spoon, remembering the funny drawing of Beatrix the Bold that the Evil Army had made.

'You know this Curse of the Wobblers business,' he said at last. 'I *still* don't know if it was true or not. I mean, it came true – you defeated the Evil Army. But Wobblers don't actually exist. Not like they say in the stories.'

'I know,' Beatrix replied. 'But we made it come true. It doesn't matter if it was true or not to begin with. We won.' She smiled, then said: 'And now I'm Queen, and everyone has to do what I say, I'm going to build a hundred gold palaces and make everyone my slaves.'

Oi put down his spoon.

'Only joking. I don't even feel like I'm ready to be Queen. What does a queen do?'

'I think you should start by capturing Captain McCannonball,' Wilfred said. 'We can't let him sail around on the Sea of Sinking Ships, stealing from people and chucking them in the sea. And the innkeeper in Collywobble-on-Sea, she's in on it too – that's why The Happy Plaice was full of fancy things. And we've got to find Esmerelda – she's the reason the Evil Army were able to take over your parents' castle. And the Evil Overlord is still at large. He has a lot of soldiers at his castle. We could fire up the Balloon of Doom, fly there and pelt him with flaming fartinpants.'

Beatrix smiled. 'Sounds like I'm going to be busy. I think for now I might just eat more marshmallow muffins and ice-cream and try not to watch Uncle Ivan dancing.' *The Beatrix the Bold Band* were playing a very catchy tune and Ivan

 was already on his feet.

'We can start tomorrow then,' Oi said, reaching for another fartinpant.

'Maybe,' Beatrix replied. 'What I really need is a comfier throne. This one is terrible.'

'As bad as riding a cart along Numb Butt Lane?' Wilfred said.

'*Almost,*' Beatrix replied. And for a moment she felt a tiny bit sad, remembering the palace she'd grown up in, and all the adventures she'd had on her way to Beluga. And even though the past few weeks had been full of danger, at least she'd had a plan. She didn't know what was going to happen in the future.

Her mother reached out and squeezed Beatrix's hand and she suddenly felt much better.

'It's wonderful to finally have you home,' she said.

And this is where we shall leave Queen Beatrix the Bold, sitting on a not-very-comfy throne in Beluga Castle, surrounded by her family and friends and looking forward to all sorts of adventures with a lot of excitement and a little bit of fear. (The fear to excitement mix is known as the 'chilli sauce ratio'. A little bit helps bring out the best in a squashed-meatball-in-a-bun. Too much and it's spoilt. Just like feeling a little bit afraid adds to the excitement – too much and you're running to the loo.)

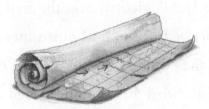

The End
(well, almost)

A few days later, a large ship with a damaged mast arrived in the port of Beluga. The captain was wearing very fine clothes and smartly polished boots. This time, both the boots and the coat were slightly too small. But despite his finery, whenever anyone came near him they were sure they could smell a whiff of sprouts.

Captain McCannonball was hopeful he might be able to pick up some wealthy passengers, and was soon advertising sightseeing trips and travel to distant lands to the people of Beluga. Because he'd been at sea, he hadn't heard about Queen Beatrix the Bold's victory over the Evil Army, but when he arrived in the harbour a messenger ran straight to the castle to tell her he was there.

Beatrix decided he should indeed get some very wealthy passengers, and sent ten of her best soldiers disguised as rich noblemen to hire his ship.

'Once you get near Devil Sprout Island, I want you to throw off your disguises, take over the ship and leave McCannonball on the island. He can stay there eating sprouts for the rest of his life,' she told her soldiers.

And that is *exactly* what happened.

As for Esmerelda, once she realised General Burpintime had failed and

Beatrix had sent soldiers from the Beluga Army to capture her, she had to abandon her carriage full of gold. It was far too heavy for a speedy getaway, especially with the snow melting and the paths turning to mud. In fact, Esmerelda discovered that no matter how much you shout at horses, when they're tired they stop moving. You can chuck as many gold bars as you like out of your carriage to try and make it lighter, they still don't move. (The only way to get them moving is with horse skis, but horse skis aren't much good when you're trying to pull a carriage full of gold up hill through slushy mud.)

So she set the horses loose, put as much gold as she could carry in her pockets and made her way to the one place she thought she would be safe. The Evil Overlord's Castle.

She shouldn't have bothered. The Evil Overlord was not in a good mood. (I mean, he was never in a good mood, but he was in an even worse mood than usual now that the Curse of the Wobblers had come true.)

'I knew this would happen!' he shouted at Esmerelda. 'I knew it! Burpintime was no good. No good at all. Whose idea was it to go to Beluga anyway? Was it yours? I've lost half my army!'

'At least you've still got ten thousand soldiers left. You can do a lot with ten thousand men,' she replied. 'You can march them up to the top of the hill, you can march them down again. Just ask the grand old Duke of York.'

'Are you trying to be funny?' the Evil Overlord said, through gritted teeth.

Esmerelda shrugged. She *was* trying to be a little bit funny. She noticed the Evil Overlord's hand was hovering over a big red button on his desk. Esmerelda, being a very suspicious person, wondered if it was connected to some sort of trap door. She glanced down, and saw she was standing in the middle of a black square in the wooden floor.

'Mr Overlord,' she said, speaking very fast. 'I know it was a terrible defeat, but we can work together to defeat Beatrix the Bold.' As she was talking she took the gold bars she was carrying out of her pockets. 'Here, take these. I'm on your side. Let me give you this gift.'

But instead of giving the Evil Overlord the gold, she placed it on the floor in the middle of the black square. 'You can use it to buy more weapons. Lots of lovely weapons.'

Soon she was standing next to a little pile of shiny gold bars and gold coins. The Evil Overlord got up from behind his desk. Like all Evil Overlords, he couldn't resist a pile of shiny gold. Esmerelda stepped to one side, so she was no longer standing in the black square. She smiled sweetly.

'Arrows with poison tips, extra long swords, spears that are pointy at both ends,' she said. 'You could really treat yourself.'

As the Evil Overlord examined the gold, working

out exactly how many weapons he might be able to buy, Esmerelda moved out of the way, standing by his desk. He picked up the gold bars, weighing them in his hand. Esmerelda reached across the desk and smiled at the Evil Overlord.

'One more thing,' she said. The Evil Overlord looked up, his face annoyed. She'd interrupted his mental calculations. 'Goodbye!' She hit the red button.

The floor opened, and the gold and the Evil Overlord disappeared into a black hole. She heard him yelling '*Aaaaarrrrrghhhhh!*' as he fell through the air. Then she heard a squelch and splat. She didn't look into the hole, but pressed the button again to close the trap door. *Honestly*, she thought. *Some people love gold so much it makes them completely foolish.*

On the door there was a sign that said *The Evil Overlord*. Esmerelda took it down and scratched her own name into it. It now said:

Esmerelda the Terrible, the Evil Overlord.

She hung it up on the door again. *Much better,* she thought.

Quiz

See how much you can remember about Beatrix's adventure with this quiz!

1. What does Captain McCannonball think will cure sea sickness?

2. Why shouldn't you sing on the *Cutty Shark?*

3. What is Oi's favourite cannonball joke?

4. What does General Burpintime want to call his book?

5. When Oi opens the chest labelled *biscuits*, what does he find inside?

6. What flavour chewing gum do wolves like?

7. How many ways are there to eat a marshmallow, according to General Burpintime's book?

8. How many fartinpants does Mrs Fartinpants make to help overthrow the Evil Army?

9. How long was the shortest battle in the history of battles?

10. How many marshmallows did General Burpintime eat during the battle?

Answers: 1. Mint 2. Captain McCannonball will throw you to the sharks! 3. *The pirate wondered why the cannonball was getting bigger, and then it hit him!* 4. General Burpintime the Brilliant. 5. Silk. 6. Strawberry. 7. 102. 8. 500. 9. 17.5 seconds. 10. 17.5 marshmallows.

How to Make a Fish Cake
(Oi's recipe)

1. First hire a sailing ship. Make sure you check it's not a pirate ship. If there's a flag with a skull and cross-bones or a long plank that sticks out over the side then quickly choose another one!

2. Sail out to sea. Try to remember which way you're going. It's easy to get lost at sea as there are no roads or landmarks to show you the way and the sea all looks like … well, like sea.

3. Catch some fish and sail back to shore.

4. If you made it back alive, congratulations! If you didn't, sorry. Hope you enjoy the sprouts on Devil Sprout Island.

5. Now, the cooking. Get a grown-up to boil the potatoes and cook the fish in the oven. Once cooked, carefully remove the skin and bones from the fish. Mash it up with the potato and an egg, make small cannonballs from the mixture then squash them flat.

6. Fry the squashed cannonballs in a little oil. (Use the same grown-up you used last time to do this.)

7. When they've cooled down, carefully remove all the fish and serve with a crisp green salad. Or with a crisp. (Salt and vinegar works best but cheese and onion also adds a certain depth of flavour.)

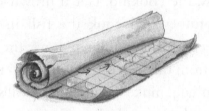

How to Play Pirate Skittles

For this you will need:
• One ship full of pirates (at least 100 hearty fellows)
• A stormy sea
• Five large barrels (the heavier the better)
• Rope to tie the barrels
• A dog to chew through the rope

1. Arrange ten of the pirates in a triangle at one end of the deck.

2. Place the barrels in the centre of the deck and tie them together. (This can be quite hard

in a storm – you may need to get one of the pirates to help.)

3. Once the ship is rolling up and down on the waves, unleash your dog and tell it to chew through the rope!

4. Bonus points are awarded if you topple all ten pirates in one go.

5. Repeat till all the pirates have been knocked into the sea!

Warning: Pirates don't like this game. If they climb out of the sea and back onto the ship they'll be **very** angry and probably wave their swords at you in a threatening manner. To make them feel better, tell them they were lucky the sharks didn't eat them.

Evil Army Dictionary

Evil Army soldiers use very few words, and most of the words are very angry indeed, but that doesn't always mean they're going to kill you or chop you into tiny pieces. It's just how they talk. The phrases below will help you communicate with them, should you ever have the misfortune to meet one. Most of the phrases should be shouted angrily, rather than spoken, but some can be *hissed*.

• BAD MORNING! – Good morning (usually accompanied by a punch on the arm or chin).

• You IDIOT! – I really like you.

• *Get out of my way* (you need to clench your teeth together in order to make it sound right) – Would you mind moving to one side? I'm afraid you're blocking my path.

The following can be used at meal times:

• Kill kill kill! – Hooray, it's tea time!

• Kill kill kiiiiiilll? – I think these sprouts are over-cooked.

• Kill kill kill – Could I have some marshmallows instead?

• Kill KILL KILL – I'm going to kill you!

At bed time:

• Sleep badly, ya FOOL! – Sleep well, my friend.

• Get me a drink. NOW! – I'd love a hot chocolate if that's OK.

• I ain't scared of the dark – I want my teddy bear!

Acknowledgements

Thanks once again to the team at Piccadilly for turning my words into wonderful-looking books. To Georgia and Jenny for the edits and Cherie for more amazing illustrations (this book has some of my all-time favourites in it!). Thanks to my agent Chloe, and of course thanks to Louis and Penelope. 'Horse skis' not 'huskies' – that one belongs to Louis.